The BIG
Book of
Pet Stories

The **BIG** Book of Pet Stories

Published by the Penguin Group
Penguin Books Ltd, 27 Wrights Lane, London W8 5TZ, England
Penguin Putnam Inc., 375 Hudson Street, New York, New York 10014, USA
Penguin Books Australia Ltd, Ringwood, Victoria, Australia
Penguin Books Canada Ltd, 10 Alcorn Avenue, Toronto, Ontario, Canada M4V 3B2
Penguin Books India (P) Ltd, 11 Community Centre, Panchsheel Park, New Delhi – 110 017, India
Penguin Books (NZ) Ltd, Cnr Rosedale and Airborne Roads, Albany, Auckland, New Zealand
Penguin Books (South Africa) (Pty) Ltd, 5 Watkins Street, Denver Ext 4,
Johannesburg 2094, South Africa

On the World Wide Web at: www.penguin.com

Penguin Books Ltd, Registered Offices: Harmondsworth, Middlesex, England

Lucky in the Doghouse first published as *A Boy in the Doghouse* in the USA by Simon & Schuster Books for
Young Readers 1991; published in Great Britain by Viking 1993; published in Puffin Books 1994;
reissued as *Lucky in the Doghouse* in Puffin Books 1999

Hamster in Danger first published in Puffin Books 2000

Allie's Crocodile first published in Puffin Books 1997

This edition published by Viking 2001
1

Printed in Britain by Omnia Books Ltd, Glasgow

British Library Cataloguing in Publication Data
A CIP catalogue record for this book is available from the British Library

ISBN 0–670–91242–5

Contents

CONTENTS

BETSY DUFFEY

Lucky in the Doghouse

Illustrated by Leslie Morrill

For Scott

Contents

The Puddle Problem

ERF! ERF!

George's eyes blinked open. He looked over at his clock.

2.00 A.M.

ERF! ERF!

He lay in bed wide awake. From the back garden came the barks of a lonely puppy.

ERF! ERF!

George said a prayer. 'Please stop, Lucky. Please stop barking!'

ERF! ERF!

By now his mother and father might be awake. They would be angry about the barking. Soon they would be on their way downstairs.

ERF! ERF!

Mrs Haines, the next-door neighbour, might wake up too. She would call George's parents and complain. She might even call the police.

ERF! ERF!

George couldn't stand it any more. He jumped out of bed and ran downstairs, carrying his blanket.

When he got to the door he eased it open and slipped out into the back garden.

The air was cool. The grass was cold and wet on his bare feet.

ERF! ERF!

He hurried over to the doghouse.

'Quiet, boy,' he whispered. 'You've got to be quiet!'

Lucky licked George's face. His little body wiggled with delight.

ERRRF!

He barked one bark of happiness, then licked George some more.

'Quiet, boy! You've got to settle down.'

George tried to make Lucky lie down. He

tried to cover him with the blanket, but Lucky grabbed the blanket in his teeth. He shook his head back and forth, playing tug-of-war.

'Cut it out,' whispered George. 'It's bed-time! You're supposed to go to sleep now!'

ERRRF!

George looked at the back of his house. He could see his parents' bedroom window. The lights had not come on.

George had to find a way to make Lucky stop barking.

He knelt down and began to scratch Lucky behind the ears.

Lucky stopped shaking the blanket.

George petted his head and scratched him under the chin.

Lucky dropped the blanket and sat back on his hind legs.

Now George rubbed his back and behind his ears.

Lucky lay down all the way, and his eyes began to close.

'Good dog,' said George softly. 'Good dog.'

George's arm began to ache at the shoulder from so much petting, but he didn't dare stop.

Every time he stopped, Lucky's eyes would pop open again.

He wondered if Lucky would ever go to sleep. When morning came, would he still be here in the doghouse, petting Lucky?

His parents would not be pleased to find George sleeping in the doghouse. He *must* not fall asleep.

He leaned back against the rough wood on the inside of the doghouse and looked down at Lucky lying beside him.

George had had Lucky for only one week. He had great plans for him. He would teach him wonderful tricks – to walk on his hind legs, to come when he was called, to say his prayers. George planned to teach him to balance a dog biscuit on his nose like a dog that he had seen on television.

George planned to teach Lucky lots of things. But first he had to work on the two most important things – not barking and

not making puddles in the house.

If he couldn't teach him those two things pretty soon, Lucky would have to go.

His parents were losing patience with Lucky.

They had been angry when Lucky had chewed the corner off George's father's new briefcase.

They were not happy about the barking at night.

They were especially upset about the puddles.

New puppies make a lot of puddles. On the living-room floor. On the kitchen floor. On the bedroom floor. Everywhere except outside.

Lucky had a puddle problem.

George's parents had given George one week to see if Lucky would work out. Tomorrow the week was up. So far Lucky had learned nothing.

George kept petting Lucky on the head.

He had wanted a dog for so long. When his parents had finally said yes, George had wanted to be the perfect master.

He really loved Lucky. He would do anything for Lucky.

He always cleaned up the puddles and never scolded Lucky even once.

He gave him plenty of things to chew on. He never got mad when he chewed things up, even his baseball glove.

And now, here he was, sleeping with Lucky in his doghouse.

What more could a master do for a dog?

He put his head down next to Lucky's warm back.

Without stopping his petting he pulled the blanket up around him.

He hoped Lucky would start to learn soon.

Tomorrow was a new day.

Tomorrow he would train this dog.

The important thing now was to get Lucky sound asleep and get back to his own bed. The important thing was *not* to fall asleep in the doghouse.

He kept petting Lucky.

The last thing he remembered was the ache in his arm as he drifted off to sleep – in the doghouse.

Boy Training

Lucky snuggled comfortably under the blanket. The boy's head felt warm next to his back. He was almost asleep.

It had worked! He knew that if he barked long enough the boy would come out. Now he knew what to do at night – keep barking until the boy came out!

His new home was fine. Much better than the place he lived last week – THE DOGS' HOME.

They didn't treat him very well at THE DOGS' HOME. No one petted him even once. And all they gave him to eat was dry puppy food. Didn't they know about HAM?

He had watched his brother and sister puppies get chosen, one by one. He had sat back and watched. He had not wanted to choose too quickly. He had wanted to get the perfect new home.

His sister had chosen the first person who walked in. A middle-aged woman with *high heels*. Lucky knew better than that. His mother had taught him the importance of shoes. High heels were bad news. Women in high heels did not take dogs for walks.

His brother had chosen the second people who walked in. He had chosen a couple with a *baby*. Lucky knew better than that too. Babies meant tail pulling, ear chewing, and, worst of all, less attention for a dog.

Lucky had waited patiently. He would know when the perfect people came along.

Finally, when he had almost given up hope, he saw the boy. Right away he knew this was the one. He wasn't too clean. He looked like someone who would run in the grass and not worry about muddy footprints on his trousers.

Lucky checked his shoes. Yes, they were just about worn out. The boy would be good for walks. Perfect. The boy was perfect!

He remembered his mother's instructions about how to get adopted. Hold tail up. Show spunk. No drooling.

He knew just what to do. Wag his tail like crazy and *wiggle*. She had said people can't resist a wiggling puppy. And he remembered – licking only, *no biting*.

It had worked! The boy had picked him out.

So here he was. A new home. A new doghouse. And a new boy to train. He would have to work fast. The boy had a lot to learn!

He would teach him to give him table scraps, and HAM. And not to snatch him up every time he made a little puddle.

Didn't the boy know that he had to make puddles?

After he had the boy trained, he would work on the man and woman.

He could already tell that the man liked him. The man had thrown his slipper at Lucky when he chewed on the briefcase. The man must have known how much better the slipper would taste!

The man was a little strange though. Every morning the man took him outside, put him down in the grass, and stared at him. What was he waiting for?

Then he would yell 'Come, come!' and chase Lucky around the garden in his bathrobe. Didn't he know how ridiculous he looked?

What did 'Come, come' mean anyway?

All in all his new home was OK. He would give them another day or two to learn.

He snuggled down again and closed his eyes. At least he had taught the boy one thing.

To sleep with him in the doghouse.

Tomorrow was a new day.

Tomorrow he would train this boy some more.

Lucky on the Loose

'George! Geeoorrge!'

George heard a voice in the distance. Far away. It was like a dream.

'Geeoorrge!'

He pulled his blanket around himself and stretched out his legs. His muscles were stiff. His feet hit something hard – the side of the doghouse.

Doghouse!

It all came back to him.

It was morning, and he was in Lucky's doghouse.

He looked around.

Lucky was gone. Lucky was on the loose.

Now what? He had to get back to his

bedroom before his mother came looking for him. He had to find Lucky. He crawled out of the doghouse.

'There you are!' his mother called from the back door.

He was caught.

He didn't know what to say. He held his breath. He tried to think of an excuse for sleeping in the doghouse.

'You're up early!' his mother said. 'You must have come out to look for Lucky.'

George let out his breath.

'Get Lucky and come on in for breakfast,' said his mother. She walked back into the house.

Relief! He wasn't in trouble.

He had to get Lucky. Where was Lucky anyway?

George looked around the back garden. He didn't see Lucky anywhere.

Had Lucky gone through the fence again?

Was he eating Mrs Haines's Japanese dog-woods?

George ran around to the front garden.

No sign of Lucky.

He thought about all the bad-dog stories that he had heard.

One time Jimmy Johnson's basset hound, Ernie, had been left alone in the house.

The Johnsons had gone shopping. They had not taken Ernie along. Ernie hated to be left behind.

While they were gone, Ernie got his revenge.

He went into Jimmy's father's wardrobe and chewed shoes. The whole time that they were gone. Worse than that, he chewed only one shoe of each pair. Then he dragged the chewed shoes down to the front door to show the Johnsons when they got back.

Mr Johnson had had to wear his tennis shoes to work the next day.

That was one of the worst dog stories George had ever heard.

But then there was the time when Kate Hinson's dog, Willie, was a puppy. Kate got Willie in the summer.

All summer Willie followed Kate everywhere. The first day of school he followed her to school. When Kate went into the school building she left Willie outside the front door. Willie barked for fifteen minutes. Then Willie found another way in. As Kate sat in opening assembly, she saw Willie walk right across the stage! George could still remember the way Kate's face had looked when the head teacher called out 'Whose dog is this?'

Dogs could cause a lot of trouble. George had to keep Lucky from doing anything else bad. Today was his last chance.

He could imagine his father pointing towards the door. 'That dog's out of control! That dog's got to go!'

George ran into the house. In the hall by the front door was a small puddle. Lucky had come in this way.

He had to find him fast!

He searched the living-room.

No Lucky, but one more puddle. Lucky had come through here.

He searched the dining-room.

Yes puddle. No Lucky.

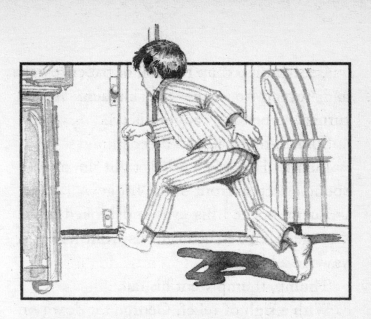

Lucky could be anywhere. He had to find him. He also had to clean up those puddles before his mother found them.

George ran to the kitchen for a roll of paper towels.

As he hurried into the kitchen he thought of all the places that Lucky could be. In his room upstairs, in his parents' room, in his parents' wardrobe, outside in the neighbour's garden, in the street!

There were so many possible places. How could he ever find Lucky?

He sighed. He had better get started.

George picked up the roll of paper towels and turned to leave the kitchen. As he turned, something caught his eye.

Something small and furry.

Lucky! He was curled tight in a ball, sound asleep in front of the fridge.

Lucky opened his eyes and looked up at George. He stretched out his front legs and yawned a big yawn.

Thump, thump went his tail.

With a sigh of relief, George sat down on the floor beside Lucky. He laid his head against the fridge door and said a small prayer of thanks.

He had found Lucky before he had been able to get into *too* much trouble.

Then he added another small prayer: Please let Lucky learn to behave himself.

Dog Looks

Lucky had found the most wonderful spot in the entire house, in front of the fridge.

It was perfect.

Warm air blew out of the bottom and warmed up the floor. The smells of the kitchen were great. Best of all the people were here.

His doghouse was too lonely.

He decided that he would sleep here from now on.

The boy had found him. He stretched up his chin so that the boy could pet him better. The boy scratched his neck.

The boy had more to learn about dog scratching. Sometimes he scratched the fur backwards. And he didn't scratch enough behind the ears. Behind the ears was the most wonderful of all scratching spots.

Still, the boy was coming along fine.

Lucky listened to the people talking in the kitchen. He was trying to learn what the words meant.

He had learned the good words first – *dinner*, *car*, *walk*, *treat*, *ham*, and the best words, *GOOD DOG*.

When he heard the words *GOOD DOG*, it meant that the people were about to pet him and give him treats.

He had also learned some bad words – *vacuum*, *doghouse*, *out*, and the worst words, *BAD DOG*.

When he heard the words *BAD DOG*, it meant that the people were about to hit him on the backside with a rolled-up newspaper.

It was helpful to know the language.

He lay beside the fridge, listening to the boy and his mother. He was hoping to hear some of the good words.

They kept talking. Most of the words he didn't understand. But finally he did hear a good one.

Car.

They were going somewhere in the car!

Dog heaven!

He loved the car. They went wonderful places in the car. They let him hang his head out the window. The air felt good on his face when they drove fast.

But would they take him?

The boy left and went upstairs. The woman cleaned up the kitchen.

He had to get them to take him along.

He thought back to what his mother had taught him. He remembered the lesson about dog looks.

There were three kinds of dog looks. All three were important. All three were useful.

The first was the 'I can't believe it' look. To do this one you stared at your people. You looked at them as if you could not believe their bad manners. It shamed them into giving you what you wanted. Lucky's mother had learned this look from a French poodle.

27

The second was the 'I am pitiful' look. This look was used to avoid punishment. For this look you made yourself look pathetic. People felt sorry for you and did not punish you. Lucky's mother learned this one from a golden retriever.

The last and most effective look was the 'I can't wait' look. For this look you pretended that you thought the people were already going to let you do whatever it was that you wanted to do and that you were uncontrollably excited.

When the people saw how excited you were they just couldn't let you down. Lucky's mother learned this look from a cocker spaniel.

Lucky decided to use the 'I can't wait' look. He moved to the back door and practised.

One important thing about all the looks was never to look away first. You had to keep staring until you got what you wanted.

The *most* important thing about the looks was *never* to blink. If you blinked all was lost.

He got ready to use the 'I can't wait' look.

When he used this look he always trembled a little and wagged his tail with all his might. Then even if they were not planning to take him they would change their minds. They would feel guilty if they left him behind when they saw his 'I can't wait' look.

He heard them coming. He got ready. He shifted his weight back and forth from one paw to the other and wiggled his body. He stared his hardest right at the boy and . . .

It worked!

The boy picked him up. They headed towards the car.

He wiggled with delight. He had done it. He was going in the car with the people. His look had worked.

Now, where were they going, anyway?

As they got into the car Lucky heard the boy say a new word and he wondered what it meant.

The new word was *vet*.

Vet!

George held Lucky in his lap as they drove to the vet's office. Lucky looked happy. He had his nose poked out of the car window. The air was blowing all over his face.

George petted him on the back. He felt a little guilty taking Lucky to the vet's after Lucky had been so excited about going with them. Lucky wasn't going to enjoy having a rabies injection.

As they drove along George thought about the puddle problem. He had to train Lucky not to make puddles in the house. He had to train Lucky today. But how?

Maybe he could learn something at the vet about dog training. It was just about his last hope.

They pulled into the car-park. The vet's office was in a little shopping centre. George's mother was going to the supermarket while George took Lucky to get his injection.

'Do you need anything for Lucky from the supermarket?' his mother asked.

George thought for a moment. They were getting low on puppy food. But after today they might not have a puppy any more, anyway.

Maybe some dog biscuits would help train Lucky. He remembered the dog on television balancing the dog biscuit on his nose.

'Could you get him some dog biscuits?' he asked.

'Sure,' said his mother. She headed towards the supermarket.

George hooked a long red lead to Lucky's collar.

Lucky scratched at the collar with his paw.

George picked Lucky up and put him down in the car-park.

'Come,' he said. He began to walk towards the vet's office.

Jerk.

The lead jerked tight. Lucky was not moving.

'*Come!*' George said louder. He thought that maybe Lucky had not heard him. He began to walk forward again.

Jerk.

Lucky would not budge.

People in the car-park stopped to watch. George's face felt hot.

Now George knew that Lucky did hear him. He was just being stubborn.

George would have to show him who the master was.

'Come!' he said again and walked forward. Lucky lay down on the pavement. George dragged him. A few feet later, he stopped.

A small boy clapped for Lucky.

George walked back to Lucky.

'When I say come, you are supposed to come,' he said.

Thump, thump went Lucky's tail.

A lady walked out of the vet's office with

a big black cat in her arms. They stopped to watch George and Lucky.

George tried one more time.

'*Come!*' he said.

Lucky rolled over on his back.

The people laughed and clapped.

George marched back to Lucky and reached down. Lucky looked up. He rolled over and sat up at attention.

He was not looking at George. His body was tense. The hair stood up on his back. He growled a puppy growl.

George saw the black cat.

The woman with the black cat saw Lucky growling. She began to hurry towards her car.

Lucky took off.

George had no idea how strong a puppy could be.

Lucky pulled George across the car-park.

George could hear the people laugh and cheer.

Lucky ran until he got to the lady's car. The woman closed the door just in time.

Lucky gave one last bark at the cat when the lady drove away. Then he sat down and looked up at George.

Thump, thump went his tail.

George looked down at Lucky. Lucky was staring at him. He looked . . . pitiful. How could he punish him when he looked so pathetic? George sighed.

'Show's over, Lucky,' George said. He picked Lucky up and carried him across the car-park to the vet's office.

The vet was his last hope for training Lucky. His week was up and Lucky was out of control.

Rabies Injection

Lucky wagged his tail as the boy carried him across the car-park.

He had just taught the boy something else. He didn't like the thing the boy called *the lead*.

They walked through a door. The boy was taking him somewhere new. It must be a wonderful place. It smelled like dogs and cats. This must be what they called the *vet*.

He wished the boy would put him down so that he could sniff around a little.

A man came out. He looked nice. He took Lucky from the boy. 'What have we here?' he asked.

He scratched Lucky behind the ears right

on the special scratching spot. He knew exactly where to scratch dogs. Lucky could tell that this was a man who knew a lot about dogs. This *was* a wonderful place.

The man carried him into a room and put him down on a small red table. Lucky sniffed the table. He didn't like the smell of the table. It smelled like soap.

The boy held him on the table.

Lucky was curious. He listened to the man and the boy talk. What could they be talking about?

Maybe the man was teaching the boy!

Lucky hoped so. The boy had a lot to learn about dogs!

Maybe the man would show the boy the special scratching spot.

Lucky decided that *vet* was a good word.

Lucky watched some more.

The man picked up something shiny and turned to Lucky.

Lucky heard another new word. *Rabies-injection.*

Before Lucky had time to wonder whether

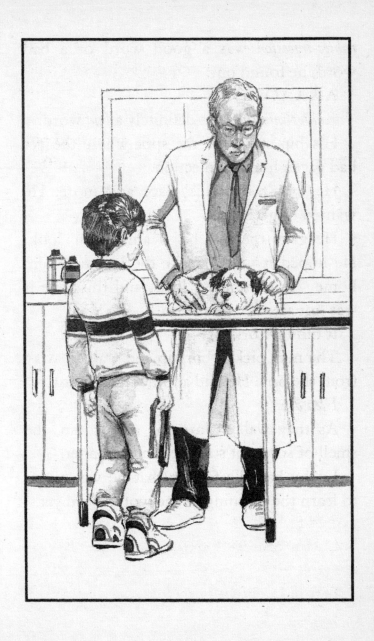

rabies-injection was a good word or a bad word, he found out.

AAAAOOOO!

Rabies-injection was definitely a *bad* word.

His hip stung on the spot where the vet had given him his injection.

He didn't like this place any more. He wanted to go home.

He gave the boy his 'I am pitiful' look. He hoped it would make the boy take him home. He trembled a little, and this time it was not an act.

It didn't work.

The man picked him up and walked away from the boy. He said another new word.

Flea dip.

As they walked into the next room, the smell of soap got stronger and stronger.

Lucky had the feeling that he was about to learn the meaning of the worst word yet.

The Good Dog Book

While Lucky went for his flea dip, George went out to the waiting-room. It would take a little while to get Lucky dipped and dried off.

He picked up a catalogue from the table beside his chair. He looked at the cover. THE DOG SHOP was written on the front. He looked inside.

On the first page was a set of matching jumpers with college emblems on them. One size for dogs, one size for people. A bulldog was modelling the dog's jumper.

One the next page was an advertisement for a dog car seat and a dog life preserver. George couldn't believe the things they made for dogs.

There was a set of dog wellington boots for rainy days. Four boots, of course. There was a Frisbee that smelled like ham –

AAAAOOOOO!

He heard a wail from the back of the vet's office. It sounded like Lucky had just been dipped. Soon George could take him home.

George closed the catalogue and put it back on the table. He looked across the room and saw a rack of books for sale. One title caught his attention.

The Good Dog Book.

George hurried across the room and picked up the book. He looked through the table of contents.

'Picking a New Puppy'

'Training Your New Puppy'

'What a New Puppy Must Learn'

It looked good, but would it help with the puddles? He read further.

'Teaching Your Dog to Come'

'Correcting Bad Habits'

'Puddle Problems'

George didn't need to read any more. This was the right book for Lucky.

This dog was about to get trained!

He put the book down by the till. He would ask his mother if they could get it when she came in to pay.

The vet brought Lucky out.

He was still wet from his flea dip. His hair was slick and damp against his skin. A few drops of water dripped from the tips of his ears. He rolled his eyes up at George and trembled.

When George took him from the vet, Lucky put his head down on George's shoulder and closed his eyes.

George carried him out to the car.

His mother was loading the shopping into the back of the car.

'It looks like he's tired out,' his mother said. 'He's had a tough morning.'

He's had a tough morning, thought George. What about *me*?

George could not remember ever having a tougher morning.

George put Lucky down on the back seat. Lucky curled into a tight ball and went right to sleep.

'Let's go and pay the vet,' said his mother.

George remembered the book. 'Mum, there's a book I need. It's for sale in the vet's office, *The Good Dog Book*.'

George's mother smiled. 'Sounds like something we could use. Come in with me and we'll take a look at it.'

'What about Lucky?' George said.

They looked at Lucky sleeping on the back seat.

'He'll be fine,' said George's mother. 'It's cool out here and we'll be only one minute. What trouble could he possibly get into in one minute?'

George took one more look at Lucky.

He hoped his mother was right.

Ham!

Lucky lay on the seat of the car, dreaming about good things to eat. He had tried a lot of good things in his life – hot dogs, a bite of roast beef, Cheddar cheese. And once he had tried HAM!

All these wonderful things floated in and out of his dream. When he got to the part of the dream about ham, his feet kicked out and he let out a little puppy bark.

Ham was his favourite thing in the whole world. Into his dream came the smell of . . . HAM. It was a wonderful dream. When he woke up he could still smell the ham.

Sniff. Sniff.

He sniffed the air. Now he was wide

awake. This was no dream.

Somewhere, somewhere near was HAM.

Sniff. Sniff.

Lucky began to sniff the seat of the car.

Not there.

He sniffed the floor of the car.

Not there.

He began to panic. Where was it!

He put his paws up on the back of the seat and looked over. In the back of the car he could see some brown paper bags.

Sniff. Sniff.

Yes, the delicious smell seemed to be coming from the direction of the brown bags.

He began to jump up and down against the back of the seat. If only he could jump high enough, he could get over the seat to the bags.

Jump.

He fell back. He couldn't quite make it.

Jump.

He tried again, a little higher this time but no go.

Jump. Climb.

This time he learned to dig his claws into the back of the seat and he could almost *climb* over the seat.

Jump. Climb.

Closer this time.

JUMP. CLIMB. OVER!

He made it! Now to find the ham.

Sniff. Sniff.

He sniffed each of the brown bags. He could tell by the smell what was in each one, but he tore each one open just to make sure that he didn't miss the ham.

Cheese.

Milk.

Uh-oh, more dry puppy food.

Soap!

Finally, HAM!

He scratched the brown paper with his paws until a little hole appeared in the bag. The smell was stronger now.

Lucky's mouth began to water.

He could see the HAM!

But it was covered with something shiny and tough.

He began to dig at the plastic. It was stronger than the paper. It would not give way.

He tried his teeth. He chewed hard at the tough plastic wrapper.

He was desperate now. The smell was so strong.

He chewed harder and . . .

His mouth filled with the wonderful taste of ham juice. One of his teeth had punctured the wrapper.

He sat back and licked his lips.

Dog heaven!

Now he had a small hole to work with. He could chew and make it bigger and bigger and bigger . . .

That Dog

'BAD DOG!'

George heard his mother yell before he saw what had happened. He peered into the back window of the car.

Lucky was lying in the middle of torn shopping bags, chewing on something. Shopping was scattered everywhere.

At the sound of George's mother's voice, Lucky jerked his head up. He cowered in the back of the car.

Worse than that, he began to make a puddle!

Was this the end?

George's mother fumbled with her car keys.

The harder she tried to open the lock, the more her hand shook.

'That dog!' she said angrily. 'That dog!'

The key finally slipped into the slot and the back of the car opened.

George climbed in and tried to get Lucky out. Lucky ran back and forth in the back of the car. George slipped in the puddle.

Every time he tried to grab Lucky, Lucky would jump away. A bag of rice broke open and the rice flew in all directions.

George's mother just stood and watched, her hands on her hips.

Finally Lucky lay down and stared up at George. George looked down at the puppy stare. This time George did not feel at all sorry for Lucky.

He grabbed Lucky and pushed him to the side.

He found a roll of paper towels that his mother had bought. He opened the roll and pulled off three towels. He began to blot up the puddle.

Lucky began to lick George all over his face.

George pushed Lucky away and began to pick up the spilt shopping.

George's mother's mouth was in a tight line.

'That dog is out of control!' she said. 'If you don't make him mind soon, he is going to have to go!'

Lucky looked at her and cocked his head to the side. George looked at her and began to work faster.

He finished his work and put Lucky over into the back seat. Then George crawled over the seat to the middle and buckled his seat-belt.

His mother was right. Lucky *was* out of control.

But why was Lucky out of control? George had tried to be the perfect master. Where had he gone wrong?

He held Lucky in his lap and buried his face in Lucky's back.

George's mother got in the car and slammed the door. George could tell that she was angry.

A tear fell down on Lucky's soft back. Lucky turned and tried to lick George's tears away.

It was too late, George thought.

Maybe his parents were right. Dogs were a lot of trouble.

It seemed hopeless.

He looked down at Lucky. This was probably his last day here. Tomorrow they would take him back to the dogs' home.

He would miss him.

When they got home, George took Lucky to the doghouse and put on the chain.

ERF! ERF!

George heard Lucky bark as he walked away. But this time he did not turn around.

ERF! ERF!

He kept walking towards the house.

Lucky had let him down.

He remembered the book that they had bought only an hour ago. *The Good Dog Book*. He had been hopeful then. Hopeful that he could train Lucky.

He wondered if it was too late. He wondered if he could ever train Lucky.

He took the book up to his bedroom and opened it. He turned to the chapter that he had been reading in the vet's office.

'Teaching Your Dog to Come'

He began to read.

> Put a long lead on your puppy's collar. Walk a few steps away, turn to face your puppy, and drop to a kneeling position.
>
> Hold out your hand and say 'COME!' in an encouraging voice. As you give the command, jerk forward on the lead.
>
> If your dog comes towards you, reward him with your praise and pats. You can also give him a food reward.
>
> Remember at all times to show your dog who is in control.

George thought about that. When had he lost control of Lucky? Had he ever had control of Lucky?

He thought about the morning, his embarrassment in the car-park, the torn shopping bags in the car, the puddles in the house.

A dog out of control made an unhappy master.

He thought about taking Lucky back to the dogs' home.

A dog out of control made an unhappy dog too.

Maybe being a good master meant more than just pats and saying 'good dog'. That hadn't worked at all. Maybe being a good master meant getting your dog under control.

George would not give up without a fight. Even if Lucky did have to go, he would try to teach him this one thing. He would teach him to come.

He put the book down and picked up the red lead.

He felt like the sheriff he had seen in a

movie. The sheriff in the movie had a showdown at dawn. He had marched out into the main street of the town to do battle with the outlaw. The sheriff and the outlaw had faced each other in the street eyeball to eyeball. Then the battle had begun.

George hitched up his jeans as he had seen the sheriff do in the movie and headed downstairs.

The time had come. It was time for a showdown.

Showdown

Lucky sat in his doghouse. He couldn't believe that the boy had left him all alone.

What was the problem, anyway? These people just didn't understand dogs. Dogs have instincts. Dogs like ham.

ERF! ERF!

He called the boy again.

How can I ever train the boy if he leaves me out here all alone?

ERF! ERF! *AAAAAOOOOO!*

Still the boy did not come.

Lucky put his head down on his paws. The boy was not coming this time.

He tried to go to sleep. He remembered the ham in the shopping bag. He remembered the wonderful smell of the ham. He remembered the wonderful taste of the ham juice in his mouth.

His stomach growled. In all the excitement they had forgotten to give him lunch.

He heard a noise. Someone was coming. He looked up and saw the boy walking across the yard towards him.

Lucky wagged his tail.

They had remembered his lunch! They had finally realized that he belonged in the house with them! They –

He stopped wagging his tail and looked closer at the boy. The boy had the long red lead in one hand. In the other he had some dog biscuits.

He was happy to see the dog biscuits, but what was the lead for? Hadn't he already shown the boy that he hated the lead? Hadn't he sat down firmly and made the boy pull him last time?

That should have been proof enough that he didn't like leads.

So now what was the boy going to do

with that lead?

George walked up to the doghouse and took off the chain. Then he attached the long lead to Lucky's collar.

I won't budge, thought Lucky, no matter what, I won't budge.

He stared at the boy. He used his 'I can't believe it' look. The boy stared back.

They stared right into each other's eyes for a full minute. Lucky blinked.

The boy took the other end of the lead and walked away.

When the lead was straight and tight, he stopped and turned around and looked at Lucky.

No matter what, I will not budge, thought Lucky.

'Come!' the boy said.

Come? There was that word again. What did it mean?

Right now Lucky didn't care what it meant. He was concentrating too hard on the bad feeling of the lead attached to his collar.

'Come!' the boy said again. This time the boy jerked the lead towards him.

Jerk!

The collar cut into Lucky's neck and pulled him down into the grass.

It hurt a little.

What was the boy doing?

'Come!' the boy called again.

Lucky began to back up. He pulled at the collar and arched his back against the lead like a bucking bronco.

I will not budge, he thought.

Jerk!

The boy pulled him forward again.

Down on the grass he went again.

Six times the boy said 'Come,' and six times the boy jerked the lead forward. Six times Lucky was pulled down on to the grass.

After the sixth time he looked up at the boy. He couldn't believe the boy was doing this to him. It looked as if the boy was getting ready to jerk the lead again.

This time, Lucky decided, he would try something different. This time when the boy said 'Come,' he would trick the boy. Instead of letting the boy jerk him forward into the grass, he would run forward *towards* the boy. Then the boy could not jerk the lead and hurt him.

'Come!'

Lucky ran forward towards the boy. When the boy jerked the lead, Lucky kept running. He didn't even feel the jerk!

He had tricked the boy!

'GOOD DOG!' the boy yelled.

Good dog?

The boy was *happy*?

Lucky loved to make the boy happy. He loved to hear the boy say those magic words *good dog*.

He kept running towards the boy. When he got to the boy the boy petted him all over and gave him a dog biscuit and called him 'GOOD DOG'.

Now he knew what *come* meant! It meant I have a dog biscuit for you, and I want to pat you, and I want to call you *good dog!*

Next time he heard the boy say 'Come' he would run right to him!

What a wonderful master he had.

The Ten-foot Puddle

George petted Lucky over and over. He gave him another dog biscuit.

What a wonderful dog he had!

What a wonderful *book* he had.

Before today George had no idea just how useful a book could be. This one would help him save Lucky, he hoped.

George walked back away from Lucky and called him again.

'Come!' he said. Lucky did not even hesitate. He ran straight to George.

George called him over and over, and every time he called Lucky he came.

Lucky *could* learn something! He had learned to come!

Maybe there was hope for Lucky after all.

He took off the lead and rubbed Lucky on the neck. Lucky rolled over on his back. George scratched him on the chest.

Learning to come was an important thing, but right now it was not the most important

thing. His father would be home soon and they had not made *any* progress on the puddle problem.

George remembered his book, *The Good Dog Book*. It had a chapter called 'Puddle Problems'.

He ran inside to get the book. Lucky followed him.

George hurried up to his bedroom and sat on the bed. Lucky sat down on the floor beside the bed.

He opened the book to the table of contents and quickly ran his finger down the list of chapters.

He turned to page 42 and began to read.

Whenever your puppy makes a puddle outside, give him a reward. The reward can be praise and pats.

Whenever your puppy makes a puddle indoors, show him that this is not allowed.

Puppies hate loud noises. One way of showing him would be with a string of tins. Each time you see your puppy begin to make a puddle indoors, throw the tins beside the puppy. The goal is not to hit the puppy with the tins but to make a loud noise beside the puppy. Say 'bad dog' and quickly take the puppy outside.

A string of tins? Bad dog?

It didn't sound nice to George. It sounded cruel. But taking Lucky back to the dogs' home would not be nice either.

He decided to try it. It wouldn't hurt Lucky, and it might work. The book had been right about 'Teaching Your Dog to Come'. Maybe it was right about puddles too.

He closed the book, stepped over Lucky, and ran down to the kitchen. He would start the training now. The puddle problem was going to be solved today, or else.

It didn't take long to find some tins and string. Within a few minutes George was ready.

He tried it out in the kitchen. He aimed for the kitchen rug and threw the tins.

CRASH! CLATTER! CLANG!

They made a lot of noise.

He hoped the noise would get Lucky's attention. He would go upstairs now and wait for Lucky to make a puddle.

When Lucky made a puddle he would be ready.

He knew the signal that Lucky was about

to make a puddle. Lucky always sniffed a little, circled three times, then squatted.

When Lucky sniffed, circled three times and squatted, George would know that it was time to throw the tins.

He picked up the tins and ran back up to his room. Lucky was still lying on the floor. He had found a baseball shoe and was chewing the toe.

George sat down on the bed and waited.

Lucky looked up from the shoe at George and tilted his head to the side.

George didn't smile. He waited and watched some more.

Lucky got up and walked out of the door to the hall.

George followed. He never took his eyes off Lucky.

Lucky stopped at the end of the hall.

He sniffed a little. He circled once. George tightened his grip on the tins.

Lucky circled twice. George lifted up his throwing arm.

Lucky circled the last time and began to squat —

CRASH! CLATTER! CLANG!

The tins hit the floor beside Lucky.

George watched.

Lucky jumped a foot into the air. He took off running. When he took off running, he did *not* stop making the puddle.

He made a long, dribbling ten-foot puddle from the beginning to the end of the hall.

Lucky disappeared down the steps.

George didn't have time to worry about the puddle. George charged after him. He remembered the second part of the lesson. Scold him and take him outside quickly.

George caught him. He looked down at the trembling dog in his arms. He wanted to hug him and say, 'It's OK, boy.' But he didn't.

'BAD DOG!' he said instead. He took him out into the back garden and put him down. Lucky was still trembling a little. He sniffed. He circled three times, squatted, and finished his puddle.

'Good dog!' George said now. 'Good dog.'

He patted Lucky over and over again.

He hoped the book was right. The string of tins still seemed a little mean to George.

It did get Lucky's attention. But it had also caused a ten-foot puddle in the upstairs hall.

He would keep trying the tins all afternoon. He didn't know how else to train Lucky.

He hoped it would work.

George picked up Lucky and headed back into the house. He had to go upstairs.

He needed his tins. And he had a ten-foot puddle to clean up.

Dog Heaven

Lucky sat beside the table with his head resting on his paws. His people were eating dinner. His people were eating HAM.

It had been a long afternoon.

These people just didn't know what dogs liked. All afternoon the boy had been throwing some terrible noisy thing called *tins* at him every time he made a puddle.

What was he supposed to do? How was he supposed to make puddles? He really had a puddle problem.

Worst of all, they still gave him only dry puppy food and kept all the good things for themselves.

The smell of ham coming from the table

was unbearable. It made him weak with desire. He couldn't bear to watch them eating bite after bite of juicy, tender, delicious ham.

He followed every bite with his eyes. His head went back and forth as the bites of ham on the boy's fork went from his plate to his mouth.

Plate to mouth.

Plate to mouth.

As he watched, the boy picked up a small piece of ham from the edge of his plate. He said something to the woman. Lucky watched his every move. He could not take his eyes off the ham.

This time the boy did not eat the ham. This time the boy turned in his chair.

'Here, Lucky,' he called.

Lucky couldn't believe his luck. The piece of ham was for *him*!

Lucky hurried over to the table and snapped at the piece of ham in the boy's hand.

The boy pulled his hand back.

'No!' he said.

No?

What kind of game was this? Was the boy going to give him the ham or not?

The boy held out the ham again, higher this time.

'Beg,' the boy said.

Beg?

What did *beg* mean, Lucky wondered.

Lucky sat up on his hind legs to get a better smell of the ham.

As soon as he sat up on his hind legs, something wonderful happened!

'Good dog!' The boy said the magic words. Lucky didn't move. He kept sitting up on his hind legs.

The boy's hand came down and dropped the ham right into Lucky's mouth.

Dog heaven!

He had done it. He had trained the boy to give him the ham. Now he knew what to do.

'Beg,' the boy said again, holding up another bit of ham.

Lucky sat up on his hind legs. He hoped the boy would not forget what he had learned. He was supposed to give the piece of ham to Lucky.

The ham lowered.

Dog heaven again!

He had trained the boy! He had done it!

He tried again and again. Even the man and the woman were pleased. The man cut off another slice of ham for the boy to give Lucky.

Life just got a little better, thought Lucky as he ate bite after bite of the juicy ham.

Better, but not perfect. One thing still bothered Lucky. The puddle problem. How could he get the boy to stop throwing the tins at him?

If I could only solve the puddle problem, he thought. Then life would truly be perfect.

The Barking Problem

George felt great. He had trained Lucky to do two things in only one day.

Lucky had shown that he could learn to come. Lucky had shown that he could learn to beg. But he had made no progress on the most important thing. The puddle problem.

All day George had followed Lucky around with the tins.

Five times he had thrown the tins. Five throws, five puddles in the house. Lucky wasn't catching on at all.

He looked over at his father across the table. He was cutting another slice of ham for Lucky. He was laughing at Lucky.

Maybe his father was beginning to like Lucky.

Maybe this was the time to ask if he could keep Lucky. George gave it a try.

'Dad,' George asked. 'Do you think we can keep him?'

'Well,' his father began. 'We had a rough start. But I see that you have made some progress with him. How are we coming with the puddle problem?'

George didn't answer. The answer was 'not good'. The answer was 'not good at all'.

There was a moment of silence.

'I see,' his father continued. 'And how are we doing with the night barking? I heard him again last night.'

George's throat felt tight. He had been so worried about the puddle problem that he had forgotten all about the barking problem. The book did not have a chapter on barking at night.

George couldn't sleep in the doghouse for ever.

Was it hopeless?

He had an idea.

'Dad, do you think Lucky could sleep in the kitchen? I know he wouldn't bark if he slept in the kitchen.'

His father frowned.

'Until the puddle problem is taken care of, that dog will have to sleep outside!'

He frowned again.

'If the puddle problem is not taken care of, that dog will have to go back to the dogs' home!'

George was silent.

When his father started calling Lucky 'that dog', it was time to stop the conversation.

George looked down at Lucky. Lucky was sitting up on his hind legs. He was looking up at George with his cutest stare.

George felt his eyes fill with tears.

He handed Lucky one more piece of ham.

Lucky had shown George that he could learn *some* things. But could he learn the two most *important* things?

People Training

Lucky looked at the boy and the man and the woman sitting around the table.

He had trained them to give him ham. How could he train them not to throw tins at him and yell 'bad dog' every time he made a puddle?

He had to think of a way to teach them, fast. He needed to make a puddle right now!

Maybe he could just avoid the puddle problem altogether by making the puddles outside.

But how could he get out of the door?

He had trained the people to give him ham. Maybe he could train them to open the door for him.

They seemed to be in a good training mood.

Lucky decided to give it a try.

He ran to the kitchen door to see what would happen.

He barked once.

The boy jumped up from the table. The woman jumped up. The man jumped up.

'GOOD DOG!' they all three yelled together. Then all three ran towards the door.

Did they ever get excited!

'GOOD DOG!' they yelled over and over.

If he had known how excited these people would get over his barking at the door, he would have done it a long time ago!

The man opened the door.

Lucky ran outside, sniffed, circled three times, and made a puddle in the grass.

They went wild again! GOOD DOG!

These people sure were easy to train!

The man ran back inside the house and brought out – more HAM!

They petted Lucky over and over.

Lucky marched proudly back into the house. At last he had trained his people! He had solved the puddle problem.

It was easy after all.

He decided that he would bark at the door and make puddles outside from now on.

It would be one way to keep the people from throwing tins and yelling 'bad dog!'

It would be a good way to keep these people trained to open the door and say 'good dog'.

Lucky lay down in front of the fridge. Everything seemed perfect. He closed his eyes.

He was tired.

Training people was hard work.

He was content. He was in his favourite spot. He was in the house. His stomach was full of warm ham. And the words *good dog* still echoed in his brain.

He drifted off to sleep. No need to bark tonight.

Good Dog

George and his mother and father gazed down at the little dog sleeping in front of the fridge. For a moment they were silent.

George's parents looked at each other in agreement.

His father was the first to speak.

'George,' he said, 'I think we have quite a good dog here. You have come a long way with him in only a week. I'm proud of you.'

George smiled. He was proud of himself. Training Lucky had been hard, maybe the hardest thing he had ever done.

Lucky was well on his way to learning to be a good dog, and George was well on his way to learning to be a good master.

His father had said that he had come a long way. Was it enough? Did this mean he could keep Lucky?

Before he could ask, his father continued.

'It would be a shame not to keep Lucky now that his training is off to such a good start.'

KEEP LUCKY!

His dad had said the words 'Keep Lucky'.

He smiled his biggest smile at his mother and father. His parents smiled back.

'Thanks, Dad! Thanks, Mum!' George said. He hugged his father, then his mother, then his father again, then his mother again.

'I'll keep working with him. I'll keep him under control.'

George bent down and scratched Lucky behind his ears. Lucky was his dog now.

He watched him sleeping.

In a few minutes he would have to take him out to the doghouse.

He scratched him again.

Lucky slept soundly, but his back legs kicked out in a little puppy kick at the

pleasant feeling of the scratch.

George wished that he could leave him there.

His parents started to walk away. Then his father turned back.

'Oh, George,' he said. 'Lucky looks so content. Let's let him sleep where he is tonight.'

George smiled again.

The barking problem had just been solved! If Lucky slept inside he wouldn't bark.

George leaned back against the fridge. Now everything seemed perfect. He closed his eyes.

He was tired.

Training dogs was hard work.

It was his bedtime too. Tonight he could sleep in his own bed. Tonight there would be no barking.

He gave Lucky one more scratch behind the ears and stood up.

Before he went upstairs to bed, he watched Lucky sleeping for one more minute.

Then he bent down and whispered two words softly in Lucky's ear. The two words that are the happiest words for a dog to hear and the happiest words for a master to say: 'Good dog.'

Elizabeth Hawkins

Hamster in Danger

Illustrated by Ben Cort

To David Hawkins

Contents

1. Yummy Rock Cakes

Luke Jones poured the sugar into a wire sieve and shook the sieve over the four rock cakes on the kitchen table. They smelt delicious!

Luke had made the rock cakes with his mother when he had got back from school. He'd mixed together the warm-smelling spices and the flour, rubbed in the butter, and sprinkled in the sugar and sultanas. Luke had left them for twenty minutes in the oven and now they were a gorgeous golden colour, with not a single burnt bit on them. The sieved sugar made the rocky peaks glisten with sugar snow.

'Those have turned out well!' said Luke's mother.

Luke picked up a cake, still warm, and sniffed the crumbly, buttery smell.

'Do you think the old folks will like them?'

'They'll love them,' said his mother. 'Why not test one out? You'll still have three left.'

'Mmm . . . yummy!' Luke spluttered, as his teeth bit into the warm bun.

While the buns cooled on the wire cake-rack, Luke settled down to watch television. It was the first episode of the brand new series *Exterminator III*.

'Mmm . . . yummy!' said Luke's father, coming in from work. 'I know a good rock cake when I taste one.'

'No, Dad!' said Luke. 'They're for the Harvest Thanksgiving at school tomorrow. We're taking them to the old folks at Hopswood Mansions.'

Before Luke went to bed, he and his mother found an old ice-cream carton, covered it with stripy wrapping paper and put the three rock cakes inside. They sealed the box with shiny cellophane. It looked great!

Next morning, the alarm shrieked beside Luke's bed.

On weekdays and holidays Luke was always the first up, but on school days he got his old sleeping sickness back.

This morning he didn't stay in bed though.

He remembered that it was the Harvest Thanksgiving. The whole class would be free of school for the afternoon, so that they could deliver their harvest food gifts.

'Anna-Louise's mother has just rung from next door,' said Luke's mother at breakfast. 'She wants you to help Anna-Louise carry a cake to school.'

Luke choked on his cornflakes.

Oh no! He'd been trying to keep away from Anna-Louise. Whenever Anna-Louise came, trouble crept after her.

'Anna-Louise's mother has been up most of the night icing a cake for Anna-Louise.'

'Icing a cake all night?' said Luke's

father, peering over his newspaper.

'She's just finished a class in cake icing at the local college, and she says this is her showpiece. It's for the Harvest Thanksgiving.'

2. To School Backwards

Luke hitched his backpack carefully across his shoulders. He didn't want to damage his stripy rock-cake package at the bottom.

Ding-dong, chimed the bell on Anna-Louise's shiny green front door.

The door opened a crack. An eye peered out next to the 'NO HAWKERS, NO VENDORS, NO

CANVASSERS, NO CALLERS
WITHOUT APPOINTMENT' sign.

'Oh, it's you, Luke.' The door
widened to reveal Anna-Louise's
mother in a pink apron, with not a stain
or a crease.

'I hope you've got clean hands, Luke.
It's unhygienic to handle cakes without
clean hands. Let me see.'

'They are clean,' protested Luke,
hiding his hands behind him.

Anna-Louise wasn't allowed to keep a
pet because her mother said pets were
unhygienic. Not even the school
hamster had been allowed in the house.

'Is Anna-Louise ready? Mr Pigott said
we mustn't be late for school today as
it's a special day.'

'Anna-Louise!' shrieked Anna-
Louise's mother. 'Come down at once!

I don't want Luke dawdling in the kitchen in his dirty shoes.'

Anna-Louise's kitchen was the sort of place you were only allowed to walk around in socks in case you made the floor dirty.

'I'm coming, Mummy,' came a muffled voice.

A white box on legs was walking towards Luke. Only a few ginger curls peeping round the edge warned Luke it was Anna-Louise.

'That box is enormous!' said Luke. 'How are we going to carry that? I've already got my backpack.'

'Nonsense, Luke,' said Anna-Louise's mother briskly. 'I've seen you with your backpack *and* a football, and your football boots. One cake box is nothing for a tough, rough boy like you.'

Luke peered into the box. The cake was round and huge. It was covered in white icing and pink curly bits, primrose flowers with silver ball centres, and twirly green leaves.

Luke stared in amazement. No one would notice his rock cakes alongside Anna-Louise's cake.

'All made of icing sugar and marzipan,' said Anna-Louise's mother proudly. 'I didn't finish it till late last night. I'm quite dead with exhaustion, which is why I can't take Anna-Louise to school.'

Anna-Louise's mother was always dead with something, but, strangely, she never seemed to die.

'What are you taking to the Harvest Thanksgiving, Luke?' asked Anna-Louise nervously, as she saw Luke's look of horror.

'Rock cakes.'

'Rock cakes.' A tight laugh escaped from Anna-Louise's mother. 'Did you say "rock cakes"?'

'I made them myself,' said Luke indignantly.

'You are lucky,' said Anna Louise.

'I've never made rock cakes . . . or cooked anything myself.'

'Certainly not,' said Anna-Louise's mother. 'I'll not have children messing around in my kitchen. Now carry the box carefully. That's right, Luke. You take the end. You can walk backwards to school.'

It was difficult walking to school backwards without bumping into anyone. At the same time, Luke had to hunch his shoulders to stop his backpack falling off.

'I'm sorry, Luke,' came the muffled voice from the other end of the box. 'I didn't know the cake would be this big.'

'It's huge,' said Luke crossly. 'There wasn't a cake as big as this in my mum's recipe book.'

'It's a wedding cake, Luke. Mummy said she must start practising for my wedding.'

'But you won't be married for years and years and years,' puffed Luke.

'I know, Luke. And what will I do if no one wants to marry me? Mummy will die of disappointment. Will you marry me, Luke, if no one else wants to?'

'Don't be stupid, Anna-Louise.'

Marry Anna-Louise? Certainly not!

Anna-Louise had been born good, like everyone else, at least so Luke reckoned, but unlike everyone else, she had never learnt anything different.

Luke knew that because he had lived next door to Anna-Louise since they were both babies.

Anna-Louise never pinched people or

borrowed things without asking, or said
unkind things about other children.
This was odd enough, but oddest of all,
despite this goodness, Anna-Louise was
always getting into trouble – and getting
Luke into trouble too!

And here it was approaching them already – double trouble!

The terrible twins, Delia and David, each holding a very small plastic bag, had spied Luke and Anna-Louise struggling along with the box.

3. Twins and Trouble

'What's in that box?' Delia asked.

'I can't see,' said David. 'Hold the box lower.'

David pushed down Luke's arms.

Anna-Louise hadn't heard. She was still holding the box high at the other end. The cake slid forward in the box with a thud.

'Look what you've made me do,'

shouted Luke. 'Anna-Louise's cake is all squashed on my side.'

At Luke's end of the cake, the white icing was like a bumpy toboggan run. The primrose flowers had crashed down into the crumpled green leaves, and the silver balls were rolling round the bottom of the box. But peeping through the squashed mess was an edge of scrumptious yellow cake.

'Oh, no!' moaned Anna-Louise. 'Mummy will die when she finds out. She spent hours on this cake.'

Delia smiled her innocent baby smile. (The twins looked alike. They both had shiny blond hair and baby blue eyes. With their wide smiles and big eyes they looked so innocent that no grown-up would believe the terrible behaviour they were capable of.)

'I know what we'll do,' said Delia.

Out of her school bag she pulled a
ruler.

'We can use this as a knife. We'll cut
off the squashed bits and no one will
know.'

And before Luke or Anna-Louise
could put down the box, Delia had

carved off the squashed end of the cake.

David scooped the squashed pieces out of the box.

'What are we going to do with the bits?' asked Anna-Louise.

What a stupid question! thought Luke, as David and Delia gulped down the squashed pieces of cake and smacked their lips.

A wicked grin spread across their sticky faces.

'Right, Anna-Louise!' said Luke furiously. 'Put down your end of the box when I say "ready" . . .'

But Anna-Louise had already dropped her end.

'You didn't wait, Anna-Louise,' yelled Luke. 'I was going to say "ready".' Luke frowned at David and Delia. 'You

should have asked Anna-Louise first
before cutting the cake. And if you
weren't so greedy we could all have
shared the bits.'

David and Delia grinned happily and
licked their lips.

'Help yourselves, then,' said David.
'Look, Anna-Louise's end is all
squashed and broken now too.'

Luke and Anna-Louise stared down
at the battered cake.

Horrors!

The icing was now a toboggan run at
Anna-Louise's end, and a delicious hint
of yellow sponge poked through the
white bumps.

They couldn't give the old people a
beaten-up cake like that.

Silently Luke took the ruler Delia
held out to him and cut carefully round

all the cracked and squashed bits.

'Have some, Anna-Louise,' said Luke guiltily. 'After all, it's your cake.'

'Do you think I should? . . . Mummy would die if she saw it. Well, just a tiny bit.'

Luke took a piece too. It tasted pretty good: rich sponge, with a gooey jam filling, and meltingly sweet icing.

'There're a few bits in the corner,' said Delia, sticking her head into the box. 'Here, we'll share them.'

They all shared a bit more.

'And I'll just tidy it up on the sides,' added Delia.

It was better than a second breakfast!

By the time Delia had finished her tidying, and all four had sucked their fingers clean, a very odd sight met their eyes.

There, at the bottom of the box, was a small piece of sponge cake. It was not exactly round, nor exactly square, but more zigzag-shaped, with a little piece of dirty icing clinging to the top.

Anna-Louise let out a piercing wail. 'I can't take *that* to the Harvest Thanksgiving! What am I going to do?'

Luke had no idea what Anna-Louise

was going to do, but he wasn't getting involved in this. Oh, no! His rock cakes were sprinkled with sugar and not silly icing and were safely wedged in the stripy ice cream box in his backpack.

Luke hadn't asked to transport Anna-Louise's cake all the way to school backwards. He'd been forced into it by Anna-Louise's mother. *This* was Anna-Louise's problem.

4. Into the Bin!

In Class Three of Hopswood Junior School, Mr Pigott was lining up the children with their gifts of food.

'Stand in line, children, while I count you,' boomed Mr Pigott. He always talked far too loud. 'Can . . . you . . . hear . . . me? Now, we are taking our gifts into assembly where we will lay them on the table.'

Mr Pigott stroked his beard as he walked down the line counting the children, 'Sixteen – Samantha, what a lovely bowl of tomatoes. Nineteen – Ben, a tin of sardines, always a favourite! Ali – baked beans, very useful! Those will keep for months in their tin. Twenty-three . . . We're four short. Who's missing?'

All the children turned to watch as four figures crept into the room.

'Late, Anna-Louise! Late, Luke! And, dear me, David and Delia late too. Did I not particularly ask you to be on time today?'

'I was helping Luke with Anna-Louise's cake,' said David, smiling his widest smile.

'And I was helping Anna-Louise tidy her cake up,' said Delia, blinking her blue eyes.

'How very kind of you, twins,' said Mr Pigott. 'And how thoughtless of Luke and Anna-Louise to make you late. Now get into line, and, Anna-Louise, you had better stand at the back with that very big box, next to the hamster cage.'

As Mr Pigott walked up to have a

look inside, the class line broke and all the children gathered round the box.

Mr Pigott stared down into the box, his eyes wide in astonishment.

'Anna-Louise, how could you?'

'It was difficult carrying it,' began Anna-Louise. 'But . . .'

'How could you have brought such a horrid, broken, dirty bit of cake?' Mr Pigott's voice rose in a squawk and his arms were flapping like some bird that had forgotten how to fly. 'I see. You forgot to tell your mother about Harvest Thanksgiving and so you sneaked off with that miserable specimen of cake left over from your tea. Anna-Louise, would it not have been wiser to come empty-handed?'

'No, it wasn't like that,' tried Luke.

'I saw the cake. I helped carry the box . . .'

But Mr Pigott wasn't listening now. His arms were flapping so much he looked as if he was about to take off.

'So Luke, *you* brought this ridiculous, great box. I might have known you were behind this, encouraging Anna-Louise.'

Mr Pigott turned to Anna-Louise and stroked his beard.

'If you had forgotten about our Harvest Thanksgiving, Anna-Louise, I am sure Samantha would have given you a tomato.'

Samantha clutched her bowl of tomatoes tightly to her and scowled at Anna-Louise.

Mr Pigott picked up the dirty yellow bit of sponge and threw the last remnant of Anna-Louise's mother's wedding cake into the rubbish bin.

Mrs Harrington, the headteacher of Hopswood Junior School, stood straight-backed in her best grey suit on the platform in the school hall. Behind her was a long dinner table, bending under the weight of tins of custard and peaches, fresh tomatoes and carrots, boxes of tea, biscuits and baskets of apples.

'What a wonderful display of food we have to be thankful for!' said Mrs Harrington.

The children sang a song about rain falling on the harvest while Mr Pigott played his guitar.

Mrs Harrington said how lucky they were to have enough to eat, and how

grateful they should be to the farmers
and the food-manufacturers.

'So this afternoon, we will take our
food gifts to the old folk at Hopswood
Mansions, who will welcome these extra
treats and the chance to chat with well-
behaved, polite children.'

'What am I going to take?' sniffed
Anna-Louise next to Luke.

With a frown at Anna-Louise, Mrs Harrington continued: 'Old people often live alone. Their children have grown up and moved away. They can be lonely. Many have pets for company, but in Hopswood Mansions the Council does not permit pets, so they will enjoy a visit from you. Now . . .' and here Mrs Harrington's cool grey eyes swept over each child, 'I expect the very best, perfect behaviour!'

Back in the classroom, Luke said reluctantly, 'I suppose you could have a rock cake, Anna-Louise. But I've only got three.'

'Don't lend Anna-Louise anything,' said Delia fiercely. 'She'll probably lose it.'

'You're right,' said Luke. 'I think I'll keep them.'

'Luke, stop disturbing Delia and get on with your writing,' boomed Mr Pigott. 'Any bad behaviour and you will not be going to Hopswood Mansions this afternoon.'

'Don't worry, Luke,' whispered Anna-Louise. 'I've just thought of something much better to take.'

5. Miss Grundy

Luke sat down next to Ali to eat his packed lunch. Thank goodness Anna-Louise had disappeared to share her lunch with the class hamster. He was glad to be rid of her.

'Did you see *Exterminator III* on telly last night?' said Ali, crunching his crisps.

'Yes,' said Luke. 'It was really scary.'

'I think those giant-legged beetles from planet Zintos are going to invade the world, don't you?'

'I don't know. I hope the Exterminator finds a way of getting rid of them. If he doesn't, I don't know how I'll bear to watch the next episode.'

'It's on Monday,' said Ali. 'I told my mum I'm going to rush home after school on Monday. I don't want to miss episode two.'

'Good idea,' said Luke. 'I'll do the same.'

'Ali and Luke!' A voice boomed behind Luke. It was Mr Pigott. 'Put away your lunch boxes and collect your Harvest Thanksgiving gifts. You two can be partners for our visit to Hopswood Mansions. Samantha and

Ben, you will be partners, and . . .'

Mr Pigott soon had the class lined up in a crocodile with their partners. The children were carrying baskets of fruit, tins of sweetcorn, flapjacks in old margarine tubs, potatoes in plastic bags. It was a walking feast.

'Where is Anna-Louise?' boomed Mr Pigott. 'Anyone seen Anna-Louise?'

Anna-Louise popped up from behind the table at the back of the class. Her face was red and her arms were clasped round her waist, beneath her school sweatshirt.

'You look very hot, Anna-Louise,' said Mr Pigott, staring at her as she clasped her stomach. 'Have you got a stomach-ache?'

Anna-Louise shook her head.

'You can't stand alone at the back,

Anna-Louise. Come along to the front.
You've nothing to take, I know, but I am
sure Luke will give you one of his rock
cakes. Now, Ali, you join David and
Delia instead.'

Luke was furious! He had been
looking forward to discussing with Ali
how the Exterminator could get rid of

the galactic beetles. Why did everyone think that because he and Anna-Louise lived next door to each other they were best friends?

As the crocodile wound its way out of the playground, Luke ignored Anna-Louise's timid smile.

Hopswood Mansions was a low block of red-brick flats. Along the flats, on each storey, a walkway led to the stairs.

Mr Pigott took the children up to the second floor. He consulted his list.

'Luke and Anna-Louise, you can visit Miss Grundy in flat 204. She has been told by her church that you will be calling today. Now remember, children, your very best manners!'

Luke felt nervous as he raised the shiny knocker on the front door. Anna-

Louise was hopping about rather uneasily too.

The lace curtain at the window edged back, and a little wrinkled face pressed against the glass.

After a lot of rattling of keys and pulling back of bolts, the door at last opened.

'The children from Hopswood Junior School!' said a little old lady with snow-white hair and orange fluffy slippers. 'Come in, come in. How nice to have visitors!'

Luke and Anna-Louise walked into a room covered in lacy material. There were lacy net curtains at the window, lacy white drapes on the chairbacks, lacy white cloths on a table and stool, and even a lacy cover for the television.

'We've brought you our Harvest Thanksgiving gift,' said Luke.

'What's that, dear? A lift? I don't use it. It's always breaking down.'

'No, gift,' shouted Luke. 'We've brought a gift – three rock cakes.'

'Three socks, did you say, dear? But I

don't wear socks. I like warm woolly tights. And three socks are not much good. That's one sock without a partner.'

Luke gave up and held out his stripy ice cream carton with the three sugary rock cakes inside.

The little old lady peered in.

'Oh dear, no,' she said. 'No, I'm afraid not. Definitely not. Those are rock cakes. Can't eat those with old teeth. Much too hard, rock cakes.'

'They only *look* like rocks,' said Luke desperately. 'They're not really hard. They're made of butter and flour and sugar.'

But the old lady sank back into a lacy chair with a disappointed sigh.

'I can't eat them, and that's that,' she said. 'Now if you had brought me a custard tart that would have been another matter. Soft pastry with creamy custard inside.'

Luke stared at his glistening rock cakes, laughed at by Anna-Louise's mother, rejected by Miss Grundy. They didn't know what they were missing.

But at least he could eat them himself on the way home.

'What a disappointment,' went on the old lady, 'and I was so looking forward to your visit. It's not often I have visitors and I get very lonely. What's that you've got, dear?'

Anna-Louise was holding out a handful of squirming orange-brown fluff.

The old lady sat up and stared. Then a big smile spread over her face, making her wrinkles disappear as if by magic.

She held out her hands and took the squirming . . . hamster!

Luke couldn't believe his eyes. But there was no doubt about it. Anna-Louise had brought the class hamster along, stuffed away inside her sweatshirt.

'My Boodles!' the old lady said. 'Oh, you lovely children! How clever of you to find my Boodles.'

6. Boodles

'You'll be in terrible trouble if Mr Pigott finds out you've brought the hamster,' hissed Luke.

The little old lady was so happy whispering and cooing at the hamster, watching it run all over her chairs, laughing as it got tangled in the lacy cloths that she didn't hear.

'Why, Luke?' said Anna-Louise.

'Mrs Harrington said some old people were lonely because they weren't allowed to keep pets, so I brought the hamster.'

'It was a crazy idea.'

'But you spoilt my wedding cake.'

'Me!' exploded Luke. 'I didn't ask to carry that stupid cake. I was doing you a favour.'

'But I didn't have anything to bring. No one wanted to share and I wanted my own gift. Look, Miss Grundy is really happy!'

Anna-Louise was right. Miss Grundy had freed the hamster from a lacy cloth and was cuddling it close.

'My Boodles. There's my sweet Boodles,' Miss Grundy cooed. 'I'll have one of your rock cakes now, dear boy.'

Eagerly Luke handed Miss Grundy a

sugary cake. She was sure to like it when she tasted it.

But, no. The rock cake went nowhere near her mouth. Instead she broke off chunks, crumbled them in her hand and fed the crumbs to the hamster.

What a waste!

Luke's sugary, buttery rock cake, demolished by an animal who was just as happy to eat any old seeds and nuts.

Soon the hamster's cheek pouches were puffed up with rock cake.

Miss Grundy stroked the hamster's head.

'Had a lovely tea then, Boodles?'

The hamster snuggled down in her hand and fell asleep.

'Shush!' Miss Grundy said. 'Creep out now, dear children. Boodles is asleep and we mustn't wake him.'

'We have to take the hamster back,' said a worried Anna-Louise.

'No! Boodles belongs to me. I lost him and you've found him,' said Miss Grundy.

'What are we going to do?' wailed Anna-Louise to Luke.

'This was your idea,' said Luke. 'Nothing to do with me!'

But Luke felt mean. He hadn't shared his rock cakes with Anna-Louise, and Miss Grundy looked so happy.

'Miss Grundy,' he said. 'Perhaps we can find the real Boodles for you. How long ago did you lose him?'

'The winter of 1980, and a very cold winter it was,' said Miss Grundy, stroking the hamster's contented head.

'1980! But that's ages ago. Our

teacher says hamsters only live two years.'

'But I *know* this is Boodles. I would know him anywhere, and . . .'

Heavy footsteps pounded along the walkway outside the flat.

'Luke and Anna-Louise,' called Mr Pigott. 'Time to say "goodbye".'

'Off you go, children,' said Miss Grundy happily. 'That's your teacher calling.'

'But we must take the hamster back to school,' wailed Anna-Louise.

'Please, Miss Grundy,' said Luke. 'Anna-Louise will be in big trouble.'

But Miss Grundy had opened the front door on to the passage. Outside stood a beaming Mr Pigott.

'A pleasant visit I hope, Miss Grundy,' boomed Mr Pigott.

'Take these children away,' said the little white-haired lady. 'They've been here quite long enough. They won't leave.'

Mr Pigott's smile faltered.

'They've not been bothering you I hope, Miss Grundy.'

Miss Grundy carefully lifted her hands cradling the sleeping hamster.

'They're disturbing my Boodles,' she said.

7. 'Why Didn't You Tell?'

It was one of those moments when they should have confessed. If they had explained to Mr Pigott what had happened and why Anna-Louise had taken the hamster, he might have been able to persuade Miss Grundy the hamster was not Boodles.

He would have said firmly, 'I'm sorry, Miss Grundy, but this hamster is not

Boodles. This hamster belongs to Class Three of Hopswood Junior School.'

Mr Pigott might have been cross with Anna-Louise, but it would have been over and done with.

'Why didn't you tell Mr Pigott?' Luke whispered furiously to Anna-Louise, as they walked back to school in the crocodile.

Anna-Louise was blinking back tears. 'I didn't think he'd believe us. He doesn't listen. He didn't listen when I tried to tell him about my wedding cake.'

That was true, thought Luke. Mr Pigott had even blamed him when all Luke had done was to help carry the box.

It was meeting David and Delia that

had ruined the cake, but then, Luke thought a bit more, he had enjoyed eating the squashed cake, and he hadn't shared his rock cakes either. Maybe he was to blame a little bit too.

'What are we going to do?' whimpered Anna-Louise.

'We'll think of something,' said Luke doubtfully.

Back at school, Anna-Louise and Luke volunteered to fill up the hamster's tray with seeds and water for the weekend.

David and Delia watched Luke fetch the water and fill up the nut and seed tray.

'There's no point doing that,' said David.

'We've checked,' said Delia. 'The hamster's gone.'

'The cage door was open when we got back from Hopswood Mansions,' said David.

'I saw Anna-Louise feeding the hamster with her lunch. It's not allowed,' said Delia, grinning wickedly. 'And she was hiding behind the hamster table before we walked to Hopswood Mansions.'

'Where have you put the hamster, Anna-Louise?' said the twins together.

Anna-Louise and Luke should have told Mr Pigott, but they were afraid to. Now they had to tell the terrible twins, but they didn't want to.

'. . . so Miss Grundy thinks the hamster is her lost Boodles,' sobbed Anna-Louise.

'And Boodles disappeared years and years ago,' explained Luke.

'Wow!' said David.

'Cripes!' said Delia.

'The best thing to do, Anna-Louise,' said Luke sensibly, 'is to tell your mum. Mums are good at sorting out difficult problems.'

'Not Mummy,' said Anna-Louise. 'She hates hamsters. She thinks they're dirty rats and shouldn't be allowed in the classroom. I expect she'd say, "Good riddance".'

'And the cake?' said David, licking his lips.

Anna-Louise's mouth dropped open in horror. 'Oh, no! I'd have to tell her about the wedding cake. She'd die.'

'Did you say a hamster is a rat, Anna-Louise?' said David.

'That's what Mummy says. She hates rats, mice, spiders and beetles. She won't let me watch *Exterminator III* on telly. It makes her nervous.'

'That's interesting,' said Delia. 'No one wants rats in their home, do they?'

8. A Plague of Rats

Luke threw his backpack on the kitchen floor. What a relief to be home!

Tomorrow was Saturday. No one would be in school to miss the hamster for two whole days. That was plenty of time to work out how to get the hamster back.

'Hang up your bag, Luke,' said his mother as usual. 'Did you have a good day visiting the old folk at Hopswood Mansions?'

'Sort of,' said Luke, helping himself to butter and jam to spread on a rock cake.

His mother looked at the two rock cakes and looked at him.

'You've got some rock cakes left?'

'Yes,' said Luke, gloomily munching. 'Do you want a bite, Mum?'

'There's nothing I'd like more.'

In the house next door, Anna-Louise's mother said: 'Was my wedding cake admired?'

'Yes, Mummy. Luke and David and Delia thought it was delicious.'

'How did they know? Did the old folk say the cake icing was exquisite?'

'Well,' said Anna-Louise, blushing. 'It

was kind of sticky . . . and . . .'

'That reminds me, Anna-Louise. I found a sticky toffee-paper under your bed. You will go upstairs now, tidy your room and vacuum under your bed.'

A big girl was in the telephone box chatting for ages to her boyfriend, so David and Delia had to wait.

'You're late home,' said their mother.

Early the following morning, Luke's sleeping sickness had disappeared. He jumped out of bed. It was the weekend and his parents were still asleep. He went down to the kitchen to pour himself a bowl of cereal and turned on the television.

After his cereal he got out his Lego box and began building a racing car.

'And that's cartoons over for now, kids.'

The jokey young man was replaced by a solemn-faced lady who read the news. After the weather, another lady said, 'And now, over to Television Hopswood for the local news. A plague

of rats has been spotted in one of Hopswood Council's blocks of flats for the elderly. Television Hopswood, reliably informed of this disgraceful infestation, has notified the Council Health Department. In the studio we have Councillor Pemberton, Chairman of Housing. Councillor, is this not a disgrace that elderly citizens are living in such filthy, vermin-infested conditions?'

Luke dropped his racing car and listened.

'Indeed, quite shocking!' said the deep voice of Councillor Pemberton. 'Why, only yesterday, the children of Hopswood Junior School visited. We are sending in our Vermin Extermination Service today. We will not rest until the problem has been eliminated.'

Councillor Pemberton had hardly finished before there was a loud banging on Luke's kitchen door.

'Luke! Let me in!' came the wail. 'I know you're up. I can hear the television.'

Luke unlocked the door.

It was raining outside. There, shivering in her nightie, with bare muddy feet, stood Anna-Louise.

'Did you hear that, Luke? Those rats will kill the hamster. What are we going to do?'

Trust Anna-Louise to get it wrong, thought Luke. 'But the hamster *is* a rat,' he said.

'Oh, no!' Anna-Louise let out a shriek. 'Then the hamster will be exterminated.'

'We'll rescue it,' said Luke bravely.

'Go back home and get dressed. Be quick. If your mother catches you in her kitchen with muddy feet, she'll probably exterminate you too.'

9. Too Late!

Anna-Louise was right, thought Luke. If a hamster was a sort of rat it would be exterminated too. How did you exterminate a rat?

Losing the class hamster to Miss Grundy was bad enough, but being responsible for its murder was terrible.

They had no choice. They would

have to go and steal back the hamster before the exterminators arrived.

'Dad, Mum,' said Luke as he stood at his parents' bedroom door. 'There's a plague of rats at Hopswood Mansions. Anna-Louise and I are going to see if Miss Grundy needs help.'

There was a snore from Luke's father. His mother sat up.

'Rats?' She blinked. 'Horrible! But if you think you should go . . . Be careful crossing the road with Anna-Louise. Bring Miss Grundy back here if she wants and if you're not back by ten o'clock we'll come and fetch you.'

Luke's mother fell straight back on to the pillow and fell fast asleep.

Unlike Luke's parents, Anna-Louise's mother was already up, wiping off the

mysterious muddy footprints on her
kitchen floor.

'Mummy,' said Anna-Louise, coming
downstairs fully dressed, 'Luke and I
are going to visit Miss Grundy. There's
a plague of rats at her flats and the
exterminator is going in, so . . .'

'Rats! Those flats must be very dirty,'
shuddered Anna-Louise's mother.

'Don't bring that old lady back here. She might have a rat in her pocket or her handbag. And stay away for an hour. I need to give this floor a good shine with my liquid wax and I don't want anyone walking on it.'

Luke and Anna-Louise raced up the hill to Woodside Avenue. Anna-Louise was quite out of breath trying to keep up with Luke.

'You're going too fast, Luke. I can't . . . Oh! Look at that!'

There, in front of Hopswood Mansions, was a large coach, two vans and a crowd of people. A red van said

HOPSWOOD COUNCIL HEALTH DEPARTMENT VERMIN EXTERMINATION UNIT.

Out of the van climbed two men in red overalls, red boots and masks. From the back of the van they unloaded red tubs labelled '**POISON**'.

A second white van had '**HOPSWOOD TELEVISION**' along its side. A man in a baseball cap was unloading a large camera on wheels, while a lady in a smart trouser suit was tapping a crackling microphone pinned to her jacket.

'We're too late,' said Anna-Louise tearfully. 'The hamster will be poisoned!'

Anna-Louise was right. If only they had got there earlier!

'Look, there's Miss Grundy,' Luke pointed.

Along the balcony walkway and out across the grass came a procession of

old folks, some sprightly, some limping, some leaning on walking sticks or a helper's arm, but each carrying a bag or small case.

At once the television cameras started whirring and the lady reporter began to speak.

'Forced from their homes by a plague of rats, these desperate pensioners . . .'

Luke grabbed Miss Grundy by the arm and took her bag.

'Where are you going, Miss Grundy? I'll carry your bag for you. Can I go back and fetch anything from your flat for you?'

'I've got everything I need, thank you very much. We're going to stay at the Victoria Hotel for the night. We're so excited,' said Miss Grundy. 'I haven't had a holiday for years, so I've packed my best dress. And I helped Mr Bludgens next door to choose a tie and I ironed his clean shirt for him. They want us to get out for the night while the Council looks for bats . . . or was it cats?'

'But what about Boodles?' said Luke desperately.

'Poodles? Dogs as well? The Council

163

won't like that; dogs are not allowed in our flats.'

A helper frowned at Luke and Anna-Louise.

'Run along now, children. You're blocking the way to the coach.'

'Boodles, Miss Grundy!' cried Anna-Louise. 'The hamster.' And she blew out her cheeks until they were fat and bursting like hamster pouches.

'Oh, Boodles!' smiled Miss Grundy. 'Why didn't you say that before? You must be the nice girl and boy who found my Boodles. He's fast asleep in my rubbish bin. He isn't bothered about bats, and cats won't get near him as the bin has a lid. He's had a big meal and I'll be back tomorrow.'

The helper pushed Miss Grundy up the coach steps.

Miss Grundy waved. 'They say the teas are very nice at the Victoria Hotel.'

The coach moved away, full of smiling, waving old folks.

'They have left,' droned the television reporter, 'torn from their homes, each with a small bag of possessions.'

'Luke, you've got Miss Grundy's bag,' said Anna-Louise.

10. Daylight Robbery

Luke stared down at the bag he was holding. It was a zip bag with pink plastic handles, covered in pink roses.

He looked up to glimpse the coach disappearing round the corner of Woodside Avenue.

'Another thing to worry about,' said Luke gloomily. 'I can't do anything about it now. We've got to rescue the hamster first.'

'We can hide Miss Grundy's bag behind those dustbins,' said Anna-Louise, pointing to a clump of dustbins at the side of Hopswood Mansions. 'How are we going to get across the lawn to the flats, Luke? There are too many people.'

'We'll crouch down and crawl behind them,' whispered Luke. 'Everyone's watching the television reporter.'

Luke put Miss Grundy's bag over one shoulder, dropped to his knees and crawled across the lawn with Anna-Louise behind him.

Anna-Louise gave a yelp.

'Don't crawl so close,' hissed Luke. 'Then I won't kick you.'

'It's not that . . . look,' said Anna-

Louise. 'There's David and Delia.'

The reporter's voice drifted across the grass as she spoke to the two shining blond heads beside her.

'And now,' she said, 'we meet the two children from Hopswood Junior School who rang Hopswood Television. During their visit to the flats yesterday, with their Harvest Thanksgiving gifts, these children were

terrified to see a rat. So shocked were they that they informed . . .'

'Look at those big smiles,' said a woman to her friend. 'Aren't they angels!'

'Devils!' Luke muttered under his breath.

He should never have told the twins, never have trusted them! David and Delia would do anything for a bit of attention.

'And where, children, did you see this shocking rat?' the reporter asked, smiling gently at the twins.

David and Delia turned, blinking their blue eyes, and looked straight at Luke and Anna-Louise.

'Oh, no!' groaned Luke.

But then David and Delia swung round and pointed to a flat on the corner, as far away from Miss Grundy's flat as was possible.

The reporter turned, as did all the watching people.

'Quick,' whispered Luke. 'Here's our chance!'

Bent double, Luke and Anna-Louise stumbled across the lawn. They hid Miss Grundy's pink bag behind the dustbins.

Luke's heart was pounding as he grabbed Anna-Louise's hand and tugged her round the building.

'We'll have to crawl along the walkway to Miss Grundy's flat,' he whispered.

The doors of the flats had been left open for the exterminator. They crawled along and then in past Miss Grundy's shiny knocker.

Anna-Louise leaned against the

passage wall, her face as pink as the roses on Miss Grundy's bag.

'Oh, Luke, isn't this exciting!'

'No, it isn't,' said Luke severely. 'If we get caught it will be all your fault. We'll be in terrible trouble.'

They listened. No one was following.

The flat looked different from the flat they had visited the day before. There were bits of lace everywhere, chewed, messed, hanging off cushions, scattered on the floor.

Surely Miss Grundy wouldn't want to keep the hamster now.

'In the kitchen, Miss Grundy said, in the rubbish bucket.'

Rock cake crumbs led a trail through the kitchen to a rubbish bin with holes punched in the lid.

'Open the lid,' said Luke. 'I'll stand close to catch the hamster.'

'I'm frightened,' said Anna-Louise. 'What if there is a real rat in there? It might jump out and bite me.'

'You shouldn't believe everything you hear on telly, my dad says, and you certainly shouldn't believe a story David and Delia made up.'

Anna-Louise lifted the lid with trembling fingers. Luke reached in and, under several lacy layers, found a warm, sleeping hamster.

'It's the hamster,' cried Anna-Louise with delight.

'Sh!'

Luke handed the hamster to Anna-Louise and she pushed it up under her sweatshirt.

'When we get downstairs,' said Luke,

'we can borrow Miss Grundy's bag to hide it away.'

They crept out of the door, down the stairs. All eyes were on the exterminators stacking up a mound of red tubs marked '**POISON**' in front of the flats.

No one saw Luke and Anna-Louise creep away from the dustbins with the pink rose bag.

11. Strange Behaviour

Back at Luke's house, they hid the rose bag behind the garden shed. It was no use leaving the bag in Anna-Louise's garden: her garden was so tidy it would be seen a mile off.

Luke fetched his last rock cake.

He took a bite and then Anna Louise took a bite.

'Mmm!' said Anna-Louise. 'It's lovely.'

They popped the rest of the rock cake, and a cup of water, into the rose bag, so that the hamster wouldn't starve before Monday morning.

That evening, Luke snuggled down on the sofa between his mother and father and watched a comedy show.

'We will be back in five minutes,' said the announcer of Hopswood Television, 'after the local news.'

And there was the lady reporter, standing outside Hopswood Mansions: 'We meet the two children from Hopswood Junior School who rang . . .'

'That's David and Delia!' said Luke's mother. 'Fancy that!'

'But who's that crawling across the lawn behind them with that great bag?' said Luke's father, leaning forward.

'That's a very odd way to behave. And
. . . don't they look familiar?'

Luke sank back into the cushions.

'It's Luke!' said his mother. 'He's
wearing the stripy sweatshirt I bought
him last year at the market. Fancy Luke
being on television! And that's Anna-
Louise. I'd recognize those ginger curls
anywhere.'

'Is that you crawling, Luke?' said
Luke's father. 'Or is it a giant-legged
beetle from planet Zintos?'

Luke and Anna-Louise met David and
Delia walking to school on Monday
morning.

Luke was so angry with the twins that
he wouldn't say 'Hello'.

'You shouldn't be cross,' said Delia.

'We saved the day,' said David.

'Saved the day!' exploded Luke. 'You made up that stupid story about the rats, called up Television Hopswood, and they brought in the council vermin-exterminators. What could be worse?'

'It was sort of true,' grinned Delia. 'A hamster is a sort of rat.'

'And how would you have got into Miss Grundy's flat to rescue the

hamster,' said David, 'if we hadn't got all the old people out of the flats for you? Luke, you shouldn't be cross, you should be down on your knees, crawling to thank us.'

In class, all the children crowded round David and Delia.

'David, you were brilliant.'

'Delia, you looked beautiful on television.'

'Well done, David and Delia,' boomed Mr Pigott. 'What an honour for Class Three!'

Unnoticed at the back, Luke and Anna-Louise unzipped the rose bag and popped the hamster back in his cage.

'Don't you ever, ever dare borrow that hamster again,' whispered Luke severely to Anna-Louise.

'Chattering at the back?' called out Mr Pigott. 'Is it only Luke and Anna-Louise who have no kind words for David and Delia? And Luke, about that bag you're holding, the one with roses on it. Mrs Harrington has asked to see you and Anna-Louise in her office immediately.'

Mrs Harrington sat upright behind a shiny brown desk. Her chill grey eyes swept across Luke's face and held it in an icy stare.

'Miss Grundy told the police her bag had been stolen. There you were, crawling with it across the lawn with Anna-Louise. You can't deny it. It's all there on the television film, bringing disgrace to Hopswood Junior School.'

Luke tried to explain how he'd never

want a bag with pink roses on it and
that he was only carrying it for Miss
Grundy, but the coach had left too
quickly.

'I'll go round straight after school,' he
said, 'and return the bag.'

'Your trouble, Luke, is that you are
unreliable. One can't depend on you.'

'But you can!' broke in Anna-Louise.
'He always helps . . .'

'Quiet, Anna-Louise! I'm talking to Luke,' said Mrs Harrington. 'And I'm not so sure, Luke, that you are a good influence on poor little Anna-Louise. I know you live next door to each other, but I think you should see a little less of her.'

'That's a very good idea,' said Luke with relief.

That afternoon, Miss Grundy was back in her flat, delighted to have her rose bag back.

'Such a shame, I didn't have my best dress for tea at the Victoria Hotel,' said Miss Grundy, 'but Mr Bludgen said my everyday dress looked quite good enough.'

'I'm sorry about Boodles, Miss Grundy,' said Luke.

'Boodles?' said Miss Grundy, surprised. 'You wouldn't know about Boodles. I lost him twenty years ago, way before you were born.'

Miss Grundy had lived so long that sometimes twenty years seemed like yesterday, and at other times what happened two days ago was quite forgotten.

'Thank you for the bag, dear boy,' said Miss Grundy, 'Although I won't be needing it now the exterminators have gone.'

EXTERMINATORS – Monday! He was going to miss episode two!

12. Rock Cakes Again

Luke ran down Woodside Avenue and all the way home.

Waiting outside his house was Anna-Louise.

'It's over,' said Anna-Louise.

'What happened?' panted Luke. 'Did the Exterminator get rid of the giant-legged beetles from Zintos?'

'I don't know. Mummy won't allow

Exterminator on the television. She says it makes her nervous. We had *The Joy of Gardening* instead.'

'So what are you waiting here for?' said Luke angrily. 'I've taken the rose bag back. Mrs Harrington said I was to see less of you.'

'But Mrs Harrington isn't right,' said Anna-Louise. 'You're kind and I always depend on you.'

Luke grunted.

'So, will your mother let me come in and make rock cakes with you?'

'No!'

'But they were so buttery and sugary. They were the best buns I've ever eaten.'

'Well . . . maybe one day.'

'But Mummy never lets me make or cook anything in her kitchen. She says

I'll make a mess. I've never made a rock cake. You can eat them all, Luke, every one, because you were so brave rescuing the hamster.'

And Luke made the mistake of looking into Anna-Louise's brimming green eyes.

'All right,' Luke muttered. 'We'll ask my mum.'

'If I give you all the ones I make,' said Anna-Louise, 'would you lend me one back?'

'We'll share,' said Luke, smiling.

Angie Sage

Allie's
Crocodile

With thanks to Ben Baker
at Bristol Zoo

Chapter 1

"Excuse me," said the traffic warden, "you can't leave this crocodile here. This crocodile is illegally parked."

Allie looked up. She was trying to unlock her bike from the parking meter outside the carpet shop. It was raining and she couldn't remember the last number on her combination lock.

"What?" she said crossly.

"This meter bay is suspended," declared the traffic warden. "That means no parking. Not even crocodiles."

Allie looked down and saw a

greenish-brown crocodile lying in the parking bay. "It's not my crocodile," she said as she clicked in number seven. The lock opened.

"That's what they all say," said the traffic warden. "Not my car, not my crocodile. I've heard it all before."

"Well, it's not my crocodile," said Allie firmly as she put on her cycle helmet.

"In that case, miss, you'll have no objection if I arrange for it to be towed away." The traffic warden got out his radio.

Allie paused and looked down at the crocodile. "You *can't* tow it away," she objected.

"Ah-ha! So it *is* your crocodile." The traffic warden looked triumphant.

"I didn't say that," said Allie.

"Well, you can take it away now and we'll say no more about it, or you can

collect it from the pound and it will cost you one hundred and fifty pounds."

The crocodile stretched its short, stumpy legs and walked over to Allie. Allie was getting very wet and wanted to go home. "Oh, come on then," she said. She pushed her bike along the pavement, closely followed by the crocodile.

The traffic warden smugly folded his arms and watched them disappear as he waited for the next meter to run out.

Chapter 2

THE RAIN WAS still pouring down when
Allie and the crocodile arrived home.
Allie squelched into the garage and put
her bike away. The crocodile waddled
in after her. It left crocodile-shaped
footprints on the concrete floor.

"What am I going to do with a
soaking wet crocodile?" muttered Allie
to herself. "Oh *bother*!"

A gruff voice came from down by her
feet. "Thanks. Very kind, I'm sure.
When I was a short crocodile I was
taught manners. Taught to make my
guests feel welcome. Taught not to

moan about them when they were in my part of the river." The crocodile sniffed and stomped off towards the front door. "I hope your mother has better manners," it said.

Allie stood for a moment in the pouring rain. She opened her mouth as if to say something and then closed it again as the crocodile slid into the porch.

"Wait!" Allie yelled and ran after it. She tried to imagine what her mum would say about wet crocodile footprints in the hall. She couldn't even imagine what her mum would say about nice dry crocodile footprints.

The crocodile waited patiently in the porch. "Why," it asked slowly as if it was talking to someone very stupid, "why did you bring me home if you're not going to ask me in? Do you always leave people waiting outside?"

"Not *people* . . ." said Allie.

"Just crocodiles?"

"Yes – no. Oh, hang on a minute."
Allie opened the door slowly and called
out warily, "Mum?" There was no
reply.

Then her brother shouted from his
room, "Gone out. Back soon. Said get
your own tea."

Allie stood back and let the crocodile
slip into the hall. "Can you get up the
stairs?" she asked. "You had better
come and sit in my room."

The crocodile stomped slowly up the
stairs. Allie opened her bedroom door
and the crocodile slid in and lay on the
floor. Allie noticed that it was covered
with fluff from the carpet and looked
very dry and dusty. The crocodile
gazed around Allie's bedroom and
blinked a little. "Where's your pond,
then?" it asked.

"I haven't got a pond," said Allie.

"Not got a pond?"

"No . . . sorry."

The crocodile looked disappointed. It peered up at the bedroom ceiling. "Do you let the rain in, then? Sort of slide back the roof or something?" it asked hopefully.

"Er, no. Sorry. Look, I'll go and get you a drink. Would you like anything to eat?" Allie asked, hoping that it wouldn't.

"Water and fish, please," said the crocodile.

When Allie came back to her room with a bucket of water and some sardines, the crocodile had gone. She sat down on her bed with a sigh of relief. While she had been in the kitchen trying to open the tin of sardines, she had begun to realize just how complicated it was going to be having a crocodile to look after. Then she heard the sound of Mum's key in the front door.

"I'm ba-ack!" Mum called out.

"Hi, Mum!" Allie shouted happily. Then an awful thought struck her: how had the crocodile got out of the house? Suppose it hadn't? Suppose it was wandering around? Suppose it *ate Mum*?

"Eek!" Allie sprang to her feet just as the door to her bedroom opened.

It was her brother. "I'd get that crocodile out of the bath before Mum sees it; she'd have a fit. It's a good one. Really realistic. Did you get it at the joke shop?" He wandered off, chuckling to himself.

Chapter 3

ALLIE WOKE UP the next morning and sleepily stuck her foot out of bed. It landed on something cold and bumpy. It was then that she remembered the crocodile.

"Oh no . . ." she groaned and stuck her head under the pillow.

"Good morning. Is it raining?" the crocodile asked hopefully. It stretched its tail and yawned. A strong smell of fish filled Allie's bedroom.

"Oh pooh! Have you *ever* cleaned your teeth?" asked Allie.

"My teeth stay clean on their own.

You won't catch *me* putting a little pink brush with silly pictures on it in *my* mouth," sniffed the crocodile, who had watched Allie clean her teeth the night before while he had another quick soak in the bath.

The crocodile stretched lazily. "I'll just go and sit in that bath thing again," it said. It shuffled around until it was pointing in the direction of Allie's bedroom door and then started moving slowly.

Allie got to the door first and leaned against it. She took a deep breath and said, "Look, I'm sorry, but I'm not meant to have crocodiles in the house. I only took you home because the traffic warden was going to tow you away. This isn't a good place for you to stay. If Mum saw you she'd go mad."

The crocodile looked hurt. "Don't want to stay," it said grumpily. "Nasty dry place, this."

"Well . . . that's all right then," said Allie.

"Yes. That's all right then. I know when I'm not wanted," said the crocodile. It pushed past Allie and headed for the stairs. The next thing Allie heard was a thumpety-thump sound as the crocodile shot down the stairs and landed in a heap on the door mat.

"Allie! Are you all right?" shouted Mum from the bathroom.

Allie rushed down to the crocodile. "Fine! I'm fine, Mum!" she yelled. Mum came out of the bathroom and peered over the top of the stairs. Luckily she hadn't put her contact lenses in yet. All she saw was a greeny-brown bundle lying on the door mat.

"*Allie*, what on earth are you doing lying on the mat in your school raincoat on a Saturday?" she asked in a trying-to-be-patient voice.

"Oh, nothing, Mum," said Allie. "Just, um, you know . . . playing a game."

"Well, you could try playing at getting some breakfast instead." Mum stumbled back to the bathroom and put in her contact lenses. There was another shout. "Eurgh! Look at the state of this bath!"

Allie sat down by the crocodile. "Phew! That was close," she breathed. "Are you all right?"

The crocodile looked slightly shaken but it picked itself up. "Happens all the time. I'll be going then. Thanks for the fish."

Allie held open the front door and watched the crocodile waddle down the path. Somehow she didn't like seeing it go off on its own. "But it can't stay here," she told herself. "It needs to find someone who has a pond and a mum who likes crocodiles." Allie closed the door and went into the kitchen to get some cereal. There was no milk in the fridge.

Suddenly there was a loud yell from the front garden and the sound of breaking milk bottles. Allie ran to the window and saw the milkman speeding off in his milk float. Then she saw the crocodile heading towards the front gate. At that very moment, coming out of next door's front gate was Allie's neighbour, Ernest Python. Ernest

Python was the head keeper at the reptile house in the zoo. Allie knew she had to do something. Fast.

"Mum!" yelled Allie. "I'll just nip over to Gran's to borrow some milk!" She threw on her coat and ran out after the crocodile. She grabbed hold of its nose and tried to pull it under the hedge beside the gate.

"Oi!" the crocodile protested in a muffled voice.

Ernest Python, who was a nosy neighbour, loomed up and looked at Allie curiously.

"Hello, Mr Python," said Allie, trying to close the gate. There was something in the way.

"Good morning, Allie," replied Ernest Python, staring down at the gate. "That's an interesting crocodile tail you've got there," he said in a suspicious voice.

"It's great, isn't it? I got it yesterday. It's a sort of . . . joke thingy." Allie tried to shove the tail under the hedge with her foot. It was very heavy.

"Funny smell of fish around here," said Ernest Python. Allie did not answer; she wished he would go.

"Yes." Ernest Python smiled a reptile-like smile. "Thought I might have found a new crocodile for our happy little reptile house. Ha ha."

"Ha ha, Mr Python," said Allie
politely. Ernest Python leaned forward
and tried to peer over the gate. Allie
slammed it shut on his foot.

"OUCH! Oh well . . . I must be
getting off to work. There're crocodiles
to feed and snakes to walk. Ha ha." He
took one last look at the hedge and
limped off down the street.

When Ernest Python was safely round
the corner, Allie opened the gate.

"Come on," she said to the crocodile, "you're not safe on your own. Follow me. I've got an idea that might just work."

Allie set off down the street with the crocodile waddling after her.

Chapter 4

ALLIE AND THE crocodile arrived at a
shiny red door. Allie rang the bell and
waited.

"Hello, Gran," she said as the door
opened slowly. "I've brought someone
to see you."

"That's nice, Allie," said Gran,
looking a little puzzled. "Who's that
then, dear?"

Allie pointed down to the doorstep.
"OH!" squeaked Gran. "Oh, my
goodness me. It's a . . . OOH! Well I
never!"

"It's a crocodile, Gran."

"Yes, dear, so it is. You had both better come inside."

"Thanks, Gran," said Allie as the crocodile slipped into Gran's house.

"Thanks, Gran," said the crocodile. "Most kind. Nice to meet someone with manners."

"Oh . . . goodness," gasped Gran. She went and sat down. "Allie dear, would you like something to eat? Have you had breakfast yet? It's very early. Perhaps your, er . . . friend would like something?"

"Water and fish, please, Gran," said the crocodile.

"Oh yes. Of course. Allie dear, I've got some tins of pilchards. They were little Tibbles' favourite. Poor Tibbles." Gran sniffed and looked for her hanky. Allie disappeared into the kitchen.

The crocodile coughed politely. "You have recently lost a loved one, Gran?"

he asked. "A much-loved crocodile?"

Gran blew her nose loudly. "Er, no. A cat. Tibbles was a cat."

Allie came back carrying a tray. On it was a cup of tea, a glass of milk, a plate piled high with pilchards and a bowl of water. She gave Gran her cup of tea and passed the water and fish to the crocodile.

"Thank you very much," said the crocodile.

"That's OK," said Allie. "Um . . . Gran . . ."

"Yes, dear?"

"Do you think . . . I mean, would you mind if . . . if the crocodile stayed with you for a while?"

Gran looked puzzled. "With me, dear?"

"Yes. He could stay in your pond. He misses his river and he can't stay with me cos Mum doesn't like dirty baths

and Mr Python lives next door and he might put him in a zoo and –"

"It's all right, Allie. Of course he can stay with me. He seems a very nice sort of crocodile."

The crocodile gulped down his last pilchard. "Wonderful fish, Gran," he said happily. "Now, if you could show me the way to your delightful pond, perhaps I could have my early morning soak."

Gran got up and led the way out to the pond. Allie drank her milk and watched them through the window. She saw Gran and the crocodile wandering down the garden path. Gran was showing the crocodile her best roses and her favourite apple tree, then she pointed towards the pond and the crocodile suddenly picked up speed across the lawn and slid gently into the water. He sank slowly down until Allie

could only see the tip of his nose and
his two crocodile eyes peering out.

"Well, Allie," said Gran as she came
back in, "I thought you said I should
get another cat, not a *crocodile*. Still, it
makes a nice change. I wonder if I
should put in a bigger cat-flap?"

Chapter 5

ALLIE SKIPPED HOME past the letter-box, where she posted one of Gran's competition entries. Going in for competitions was Gran's hobby. The last thing she had won was a plastic seagull which lit up and sang the birdie song.

Allie was in the kitchen, putting the carton of milk that Gran had given her into the fridge, when her mum appeared. "Oh good, Allie, you've got some milk. There's broken bottles and milk all over the path. If you ask me, that Ernest Python has something to do with it. I've just caught him ferreting around under the hedge by the gate."

"Have some cornflakes, Mum." Allie did not want to talk about Ernest Python or broken milk bottles.

"Allie!" her brother burst into the kitchen. "Can I borrow your crocodile?"

"Don't be silly, Alan," said Mum. "Sit down and have some breakfast."

Allie gave her brother a kick. "Shut up about crocodiles, will you?" she hissed.

"Oh, excuse me for speaking," said Alan. "You can keep your silly crocodile to yourself then. I'll borrow Pete's dinosaur." He got up from the table. "It's inflatables day at the pool today, Mum. I'm off now. Want to get there early."

"That's nice, dear. What are you doing today, Allie?" asked Mum.

"Going to the pool with Emily." Allie

stuck her tongue out at Alan. "But we're not going near any silly boys. I'm going back to see Gran first. I want to see how the croc– um . . . how she is."

After breakfast Allie rushed back to Gran's. She let herself in through the side gate and went straight into the garden. The crocodile was in exactly the same place as he had been when she had left him. "How's the pond?" Allie asked him. The crocodile blew a few bubbles and sank down a little further.

Gran came out into the garden. "I think he's sleeping, Allie," she whispered. "He said he didn't get much sleep last night." Gran smiled a soppy smile. "He's lovely, isn't he?"

Allie grinned. "I knew you'd like him, Gran. Can he stay?"

"Of course he can, Allie. I'd be lonely without him. I'll feel much safer at

night knowing that there's a crocodile in my garden." Gran put her arm around Allie. "Now how about a nice glass of orange juice?"

"Sorry, Gran. I've got to meet Emily. We're going swimming."

The water in the pond suddenly bubbled up and the crocodile stuck his head out. "Swimming?" he asked. "I'll come with you."

"You can't," said Allie. "We're going to the swimming pool. It will be full of people. I can't take a crocodile into a swimming pool full of people."

"Why not?" asked the crocodile.

"Well . . ." Allie did not want to say anything that might hurt the crocodile's feelings.

"Because you think I'd eat them. That's it, isn't it?" The crocodile thumped his tail crossly and half the pond landed on Gran.

"Oooh!" she squeaked.

"Sorry, Gran," said the crocodile. He looked at Allie. "Well, I don't eat people. They taste *disgusting*. My great aunt ate one once and she was ill for days. Anyway, it would be very bad manners."

"But no one would let you into the pool," said Allie. "They don't allow crocodiles."

Gran looked at the crocodile

thoughtfully. "I hear it's inflatables day today," she said. "I'm sure if you didn't mind pretending to be an . . . er . . . a . . ." Gran stopped as she saw the crocodile's expression.

"Pretend to be one of those ridiculous plastic blow-up crocodiles?" he snapped.

"Er . . . yes," faltered Gran. "Not that you look anything like that of course. You are much, much better looking."

"All right then," said the crocodile.

Allie was amazed. "You mean you're going to be my inflatable for the day? That's great. I was going to have to share Emily's."

"Why not?" sighed the crocodile. "The things a crocodile has to do nowadays just to get a decent swim."

Chapter 6

GRAN WAVED GOODBYE as Allie and the crocodile walked happily down the street. The crocodile started to trot, and his scaly feet made a clicketty-clattery sound on the pavement.

"Slow down," Allie called out after him. "You're meant to be an inflatable, remember?"

"There's no need to be rude," snapped the crocodile.

Allie and the crocodile made their way to the swimming pool. Outside was a crowd of noisy people carrying all kinds of inflatables. Emily was waiting

227

for Allie by the entrance. She was holding a huge pink elephant.

"Hi, you," grinned Emily. She looked at the crocodile and her eyes widened. "Hey, that's a brill inflatable. Where d'you get it?"

"Oh. Um, I got it in town. Yesterday. Let's go in, shall we?"

They bought their tickets and headed off to the changing rooms only to be stopped by the loud voice of an attendant.

"No inflatables in the changing rooms, please. Put them over there and pick them up when you're changed." The attendant pointed to a huge pile of blown-up ducks, submarines, hamburgers and hippos.

"What?" said Allie.

"Put that crocodile over there, please," said the attendant. "And that elephant."

The crocodile stared at the pile of coloured plastic. "He wants *me* to go *there*?"

"Yes," whispered Allie. "*Please*. We won't be long."

"*ME* . . . in a pile of plastic rubbish? You must be joking."

Emily had already dumped her elephant on to the pile. "Come on, Allie," she yelled as she disappeared into the changing rooms.

Allie got tough with the crocodile. "Look," she hissed, "either you get in that pile or you don't go swimming. It's up to you."

The crocodile shuffled off and sat between a dinosaur and a banana. He looked . . . well . . . snappy, thought Allie as she raced off after Emily.

Allie had never put on her swimming costume so quickly. She dashed out and collected the crocodile.

"What happened to that dinosaur – and that banana?" she asked him. They looked suspiciously flat.

"My teeth slipped. Can we *swim* now?"

Allie decided that the sooner the crocodile was in the pool the better. They paddled through the footbath – "Eurgh!" complained the crocodile as the water went up his nose – and then Allie jumped straight in. As she surfaced, the crocodile slipped into the water with a graceful swoop. He curved down to the bottom of the pool and then came up beside her.

"Wonderful. Deep water. Mmmm . . . tastes funny. Tastes of humans and . . . ?"

"Chlorine," explained Allie.

"Ah," mumbled the crocodile. "I prefer fish myself."

It was great for a while. Emily and Allie splashed around and fell off

Emily's elephant while the crocodile swam quietly beneath them.

"You'll lose your crocodile if you're not careful," said Emily. "You ought to keep hold of it. Those boys are after it – look."

Allie looked. It was her brother and his horrible friends. Bother!

Her brother swam up. "Lend us your crocodile. Pete's dinosaur's got these massive holes in it. So has Greg's banana."

"No," said Allie. "Go away."

Her brother's friends splashed around.
There were lots of them. They circled
around Allie and Emily like a group of
hungry sharks.

"Give it to me, Allie. It's not fair. We
haven't got any inflatables and you
girlies have got one each."

"Don't call me a girlie. Go away,
Alan." Allie splashed him.

Suddenly one of the boys grabbed
Emily's elephant. "OI!" yelled Emily,

and plunged after it. Alan grabbed
Allie to stop her helping Emily and the
boys piled on to the elephant. It began
to sink . . . and then, *whoosh*, it was
flying. Emily's elephant shot up into the
air and the boys tumbled off to find
themselves staring into the open jaws of
a crocodile. SNAP! went the crocodile.
SNAP, SNAP, SNAP!

"Help!" yelled Alan.

A loud whistle blew and the lifeguard ran over. "You!" he yelled at Allie. "You with the unhygienic inflatable – OUT!"

"But it was their fault," protested Allie, looking around for the boys. They were nowhere to be seen. There was only Alan who had gone a strange greenish colour and was hanging on to the side of the pool. Then Allie remembered the snapping sounds. "You didn't . . . you *haven't* . . . ?" she whispered to the crocodile.

"OUT!" said the lifeguard. He blew his whistle again. The crocodile swam to the steps at the shallow end and Allie followed him. They slowly got out of the pool.

"No, I did not," muttered the crocodile. "I told you, I don't eat humans. They're over there – look."

Allie looked and saw a shaky huddle of boys in the corner of the shallow end. "I bet they never knew they could swim so fast," she giggled.

Later, on the way home, the crocodile said, "I don't suppose we'll be going back to the swimming pool, will we?"

"No," said Allie, "I don't suppose we will."

"Humph," grunted the crocodile. "Where am I going to get a decent swim then?"

Chapter 7

IT WAS A cross crocodile that arrived back at Gran's house with Allie. "I'm going to my pond," he said. "I do not wish to be disturbed."

Allie watched the crocodile slip off to the back garden, then she let herself into Gran's house.

"Allie, is that you?" Gran's voice sounded strangely muffled.

"Where are you, Gran?" Allie called.

"In here, dear. I'm a bit stuck . . ."

Allie went into the sitting room. A large yellow duck was sitting on the sofa. "*Gran?*" gasped Allie.

"Thank goodness you're back, Allie," said the duck. "I can't get my head off."

Allie grabbed hold of the huge yellow fluffy head and pulled hard. It flew off with a *pop!* and Allie tumbled back on to the carpet.

"Gran, what *are* you doing?" asked Allie.

"Marjorie phoned, dear. Asked me to a fancy dress party tonight. Well, I told her I didn't want to go, but you know what Marjorie is like. Won't take no for an answer. So I went down to the fancy-dress-hire place and this was the only thing they had left." Gran sat on the edge of the sofa, her flushed face peeping out of the fluffy yellow costume.

"You look lovely, Gran," said Allie.

"No, I don't. I look daft. I can't go out on my own looking like this."

"But no one will know it's you," said Allie.

"*I* know it's me," said Gran. "I'm not going."

Allie helped Gran out of the duck suit. It was ages since Gran had been out and had fun, thought Allie. Ever since that terrible morning when Tibbles had fallen into the dust cart, Gran had stayed at home feeling sad. Allie had an idea, but first she needed to talk to the crocodile.

Gran was getting some fish out of the freezer when the crocodile pattered into the kitchen. "Hello, dear," smiled Gran. "It's hake today. That all right?"

"Lovely, thank you, Gran," said the crocodile. "My favourite, in fact."

"I thought cod was your favourite, dear," said Gran, putting six large fish into a bowl of cold water.

"Anything defrosted by you is my favourite, Gran," said the crocodile. Gran giggled and patted him on the nose.

The crocodile coughed and shuffled his feet a little nervously.

"Gran," he said, "I would consider it a great honour to accompany you to the fancy dress party tonight. May I say that, apart from fish, ducks are my favourite things."

Gran stared at the crocodile. She had a fish in each hand and a strange expression on her face. "You – you'd like to come to the fancy dress party? With me?"

"I can think of nothing I would like better, Gran," said the crocodile, "apart from a quick dip in the boating lake on the way home."

Allie stuck her head around the kitchen door. "Are you going then, Gran?" she asked.

Gran grinned. "Well, I don't think I've ever been asked out by a crocodile before. I'd love to go. Thank you."

The crocodile thumped his tail and looked pleased.

"But what are you going to dress up as?" Gran asked him.

"That's easy," laughed Allie. "A crocodile!"

"I'll have a bow tie, thank you," said the crocodile. "One must make an effort, don't you think?"

"Quite right," said Gran. "I'll go and sort out that duck suit right now."

Chapter 8

IT WAS GETTING dark when three
strange figures slipped out of Gran's
front gate. The smallest one walked
between the two large lumpy ones. "I
feel silly, Gran," it said as it tried to
keep up with a big duck and a
crocodile.

"You look lovely, dear," said the duck.
"I'm so glad I came across my old
teapot costume. I won first prize in that
when I was in the Brownies, you know."

"Yes, I *know*, Gran," sighed the small
pink teapot.

The party was in full swing when they

244

arrived. The crocodile, who had decided to stand upright for the night, took Gran's arm and escorted her inside. They disappeared into the crowd and left Allie standing by the door.

"Oh great," muttered Allie. "A load of old people all dressed up in silly clothes. Lovely."

"Hi, one lump or two?" a voice laughed in her ear.

Allie turned her head (not an easy thing to do inside a teapot) and saw a small purple fairy grinning at her. "Emily! What are *you* doing here?"

"Same as you," said Emily. "I'm looking completely stupid. Who made you come like *that*?"

"Gran," shouted Allie above the noise of the music, which someone had just turned up. "What about you?"

"Mum," shouted Emily. "She's here

with her friends. Mrs Python. And Mr
Python. Silly old bat. Not Mum. I
mean Mrs Python. This was her idea.
What a NOISE!"

"WHAT?" yelled Allie.

Someone had just turned the music
up even louder and everyone in the
room seemed to be stepping back,
leaving a space in the middle. This was
not good news for a small teapot, which
got stuck between a huge gorilla, a
penguin and a horrible fat snake. Allie
could not move; she had to stand and
watch as two dancers took to the floor,
a duck and a crocodile. Everyone
clapped as the crocodile twirled the
duck around and around. There were
"oohs" and "aahs" as the music got
faster and the crocodile thumped his
tail in time with the beat while the
duck deftly skipped around him. No
one had ever seen anything like it

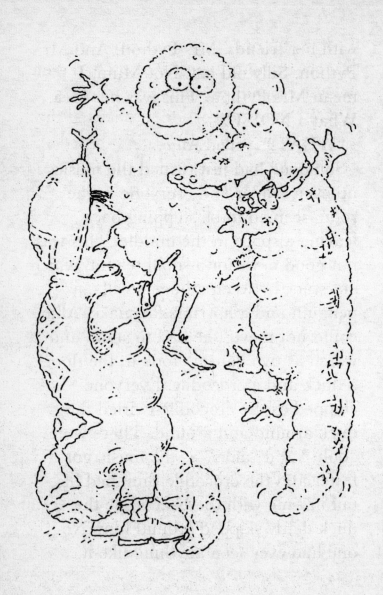

before. No one, that is, except for Ernest Python. Ernest Python had seen lots of crocodiles before.

"OI! That's a crocodile!" shouted the fat snake next to Allie. Allie jumped. The snake was Ernest Python. His voice was so loud it could be heard above the music. People laughed. "Well done, Ernest. Glad to see you've learnt something after all those years at the reptile house!" The fat snake pushed forward towards Gran and the crocodile. He pushed up his snake head so that his mean little eyes could see the crocodile more clearly. Then he poked the crocodile in the ribs. The crocodile swung round and stared at Ernest Python.

"You're a crocodile," declared Mr Python. Everyone burst out laughing. Ernest Python began to get agitated. "It IS!" he shouted. "THAT is a

REAL crocodile. It should be in a ZOO!"

Suddenly the music stopped and everything went quiet. All eyes were on Ernest Python and the crocodile.

The crocodile began to thump his tail. He looked cross.

"Take your head off then," shouted Ernest Python excitedly in his high, whiny voice. "Let's see who you are."

People at the party began to mumble. "Well, he's right, you know, it *does* look like a crocodile." "Look at that tail. It looks real enough to me." "D'you think it'll bite?"

Meanwhile, Allie had been desperately trying to get out of her teapot. She *had* to do something. Finally she pushed up the lid and wriggled out, leaving it behind her, stuck between the gorilla and the penguin. She dashed over to Gran and the crocodile.

"Gran," she yelled, "I'm going to be SICK!"

Gran knew at once that this was her chance to get the crocodile out of the room safely. She grabbed the crocodile in one hand and Allie in the other and said in a very loud voice, "Come on, Allie – you can be sick in the garden, dear." Allie, Gran and a reluctant crocodile fled down the garden path.

"I was enjoying that, Gran," complained the crocodile. "It's a shame to leave now; you're a lovely dancer."

"And Ernest Python is a nasty busybody," said Gran. "You'll end up in the zoo if he has his way."

The crocodile was very quiet after that.

Chapter 9

ALLIE SKIPPED ON ahead, down the road that led to the park and the boating lake. Gran and the crocodile walked slowly behind and it wasn't until they had reached the edge of the boating lake that the crocodile said something: "SWIM . . . WATER . . . FISH."

He got down on to his tummy and his short legs paddled him into the lake with a gentle *splash*. Allie and Gran watched the dim crocodile-shape disappear into the night as he dived down into the muddy water of the boating lake.

Allie and Gran sat quietly on a bench by some old canoes, listening to the strange sounds of the night.

Quack, quack, *quack*! A flurry of ducks skidded along the water and hurtled into the safety of the bushes. Then there was a loud SPLASH! and a dull thump as all the boats on the other side of the lake rocked and moved on the water. Allie was sure she heard the shrill cry of a small furry animal. "Gran," she whispered, "what's he *doing*?"

Gran wriggled about in her rather scratchy duck costume and managed to get the duck head off.

"Don't worry, dear," she said. "He's just enjoying his swim."

"*Swimming* in the boating lake is prohibited . . . er, madam," said a loud voice behind them.

"Aargh!" screamed Gran. "Who's that?"

"I am the park keeper, madam. Persons swimming in the boating lake are prohibited under Section Three C Subsection Two of the Municipal Parks by-laws." The park keeper stared disapprovingly at Gran in her fluffy duck costume.

Gran stood up, folded her yellow fluffy wings and stared back crossly at the park keeper. "There aren't any *persons* swimming in the boating lake," she said. But the park keeper did not hear her. He was too busy staring at the sleek, dark shape of the crocodile as he cut through the still water on his way back to Gran.

The park keeper gave a small, strangled squeak as the crocodile slid out on to the bank and waddled over to Gran as fast as he could. "Are you all right, Gran?" puffed the crocodile. "I thought I heard you scream."

"Weeoorgh . . ." moaned the park keeper. He jumped into a canoe and paddled away as fast as any park keeper has ever paddled across a boating lake.

Gran patted the crocodile on the nose. "I'm fine, thank you. Perhaps we

should go home now. Did you have a nice swim, dear?"

"Fair to middling, thank you, Gran. Very muddy and no fish. Plenty of ducks, though. Nice voles, too."

"You *didn't –*" said Allie accusingly.

"Come on now, Allie," said Gran. "If you don't ask about ducks and voles, I won't ask about teapots. Particularly a large pink one that someone has left somewhere. OK?"

"That's different," mumbled Allie.

"What did you say, dear?"

"Nothing, Gran."

Allie, Gran and the crocodile walked slowly home along the high street. Suddenly the crocodile stopped in front of the travel agent. He was staring at a poster. On the poster was a picture of a beautiful river, with crocodiles basking on its banks. The words on the poster said:

FLY TO AFRICA,
HOME OF THE CROCODILE.
Flights available. Enquire within.

Gran joined the crocodile as he gazed at the poster. The crocodile sighed a big sigh and said, "I want to go home, Gran. I want to go back to my river."

Gran put her arm around the crocodile. "I know," she said sadly.

"I don't want to leave you, Gran. I love staying with you, but I've got to have somewhere to swim. You understand that, don't you?" The crocodile sniffed a little. So did Gran.

"I understand, dear," she said. "We'll get you a ticket tomorrow."

Chapter 10

ALLIE STAYED THE night at Gran's house. When she woke up the next morning in the little spare bedroom she drew back the curtains and looked out of the window. The crocodile was dozing in the pond. Allie gazed at him, watching him blow bubbles up to the surface of the water, and watching his tail slowly flick from side to side. "I wish he didn't want to go home," she thought sadly.

After breakfast, Allie helped Gran wash up. "I thought we had better go down to the travel agent," sighed Gran.

"We did promise to book a plane ticket for him."

Allie put the last plate away. "I know, Gran. I'll miss him, though."

"Not as much as I will," said Gran. "We had such fun last night; he's such a lovely dancer. And so charming, so polite. I feel really safe with him in the back garden." Gran sighed and shook her head. "But he can't stay here without somewhere proper to swim. Come on, Allie, let's go and buy him a ticket back to his river."

The poster was still in the travel agent's window.

"In we go, then," said Gran. She marched up to a rather nervous young man sitting behind a large computer. It was his first day at work.

"I want to book a flight to Africa, home of the crocodile, just like your poster in the window says," said Gran.

The young man looked relieved. This was something he knew how to do. "Fine," he said as he fiddled with the keyboard. "When are you planning to go?"

"Oh, it's not for *me*, it's for a crocodile. He wants to go home as soon as possible."

"The first flight we have is tomorrow . . . er, excuse me, *who* did

you say it was for?" The young man
went a little pink.

"A crocodile. Tomorrow would be
fine," said Gran. The pink young man
swallowed nervously.

"Er . . . Do you mind if I just make a
phone call?" he gulped.

"Of course not, dear," said Gran.

The young man's hand shook as he
tapped out the numbers on his phone.

"Is that the zoo? Could you put me through to the reptile house, please?" he said in a whisper.

Gran nudged Allie, who was gazing at pictures of sandy beaches, and pulled her over to listen to the phone call.

"Yes . . . yes, I see," the young man was saying. "What? Lasso its tail? Oh, I see . . . and its head . . . yes . . . you put its head into a sack . . . oh . . . tranquillized . . . yes, in a very small crate so it can't break out . . . yes, yes, I'll ask. Thank you for your help, Mr Python." The young man put the phone down.

"It will have to go by air freight," he said. "We'd be very happy to arrange the crate for you."

"The *crate*?" spluttered Gran.

"Yes. Does the crocodile have an identification microchip?" the young man asked.

"A *what?*" said Gran.

"No? Well, it will need one of those. The zoo will be able to inject that."

"Inject?" gasped Allie. "He's got to have an *injection?*"

"Yes. And a certificate because he – er – the crocodile is an endangered species."

"I'm not surprised," muttered Gran, "if you treat them like that."

"Pardon?" said the young man, who was very pink by now. He wondered if this was a strange test that his boss had set him. He didn't think it was a fair test, not crocodiles on his first day.

"W-well," he stammered, "w-we can make all the arrangements for you if you could just give me the name of the z-zoo where the crocodile is kept."

"He's not in a zoo," snapped Gran, "he's in my pond." The phone fell out of the young man's hand and clattered on to the floor. He wasn't pink any more, he was pale grey.

Allie tugged at Gran's jacket. "Come on, Gran," she said, "let's go."

Gran nodded and allowed Allie to pull her out of the travel agent as the young man slid on to the floor with a thump.

Gran and Allie walked home silently. Gran was the first one to speak. "Well, are you going to tell him or am I?" she said.

"Tell him what exactly, Gran?"

"Tell him that he has to have an injection, that they are going to lasso him and stuff a sack over his head, tell him that he has to go in a *crate* . . ."

"You can tell him, Gran," said Allie.

Chapter 11

THE CROCODILE WAS waiting for them
when they got back. He was lying
quietly on the front lawn with his eyes
slowly opening and closing. He had
been dreaming of his river, dreaming of
diving down into the cool dark shadows
of the water, of basking in the gently
flowing current. He was woken up with
a start by the clang of the garden gate
as Allie slammed it shut.

"Oh!" said Gran. "I didn't expect to
see you there."

"Ah . . . hello, Gran," yawned the
crocodile as he remembered where he

269

was. "Did you get my plane ticket?"

"Er, no," said Gran. "I . . . um . . . Allie, you tell him."

The crocodile looked up suspiciously. "Tell him what?" he asked.

No one said anything. The crocodile thumped his tail crossly. "Tell him *what?*"

"Yougottogoinacrate," said Allie all in a rush.

The crocodile blinked. "A . . . *CRATE?*" he said slowly.

"Yes," said Allie.

The crocodile thumped his tail again. "I am NOT going in a crate. I came over rolled up in a smelly old carpet and I am going back in a proper seat. I want to watch the film. I want my lunch on one of those plastic trays and my duty-free drinks and I want to go and see the pilot in the cockpit."

With that, the crocodile lifted his

tummy off the ground and stood up. "I am going to sit in my pond. Oh, Gran, there's a letter for you there. The postman dropped it when he ran away. I tried to tell him to leave the post with me but he just made this strange noise. Funny chap." The crocodile disappeared off into the back garden.

"Oh deary deary dear," muttered Gran as she picked up the letter. "What are we going to do?"

"How about a cup of tea, Gran?" said Allie.

Gran was reading the letter when Allie brought in the tea.

"Bother!" said Gran. "I haven't won the car. I've only won second prize."

Allie was excited. "You mean you've won a *prize*? What is it, Gran?"

"Don't go getting excited, dear. It's something boring to do with the

garden. Here, you have a look." Gran passed the letter over to Allie.

Allie read it out: "'Congratulations! You have WON second prize in the Name That Pilchard competition sponsored by Pook's Prime Pilchards. You have WON, courtesy of Pook's Prime Pilchards, a complete *new look* for your garden! But most exciting of all, you have WON *one hundred boxes* of our Brand New Prime Pilchard Jelly (a new concept in puddings).'"

"Wow, Gran, that's great!" said Allie.

"But I wanted the first prize. It was a lovely car," grumbled Gran, "and I don't know *where* we're going to put all those boxes of that disgusting Pilchard Jelly either. I've got enough to worry about with that poor crocodile."

Allie gazed out of the window at the crocodile in the pond. She wished Gran wasn't so worried about him. She

wished he had somewhere nice to swim
so that he could stay with Gran. She
wished the whole garden was a pond
big enough and deep enough for him to
live in. She wished . . . "Gran!"
shouted Allie.

"Ooh! What dear? You made me
jump," said Gran.

"Gran, *Gran*! I've got this great idea!"
Allie jumped up and dragged Gran
over to the window. "Look!" she said.

"Yes, dear, that lovely crocodile in his
tiny pond, and somehow we have to get
him home."

"No, we don't, Gran. He can stay
here now! With your prize we can make
the whole garden into the biggest pond
ever!"

Chapter 12

POOK'S PRIME PILCHARDS had never
heard anything like it. "You want *what*,
madam?" the Pilchard person
spluttered at the other end of the
phone.

"I want", repeated Gran, "my entire
garden made into a lake. I want one
large island and two small ones. I want
underwater rocks and a small creek
and – er, hang on a minute, please . . .
what did you say, dear?" she whispered
to the crocodile. "Oh yes, fish. Lots of
fish. Got that?"

"But, madam," objected the Pilchard

276

person, "we were only expecting to plant a few shrubs, maybe dig up a few weeds. I suppose we could run to a gazebo. Can I tempt you with a gazebo, madam?"

"No," snapped Gran, "you can't. Now you get straight over here and start digging. Goodbye."

The Pilchard people got straight over and started digging. The crocodile moved into the bathroom and, although Allie ran him plenty of deep baths, he spent most of the time gazing out of the window, watching as his own lake began to take shape.

It was an exciting evening two weeks later when Pook's Pilchards drove their diggers away. Gran gazed at the muddy mess that had once been her garden.

"Well," she sighed, "it will all be worth it once I see that crocodile swimming around."

Allie clambered into the dry lake. She ran down to the deepest part in the middle and looked up. It was so deep that she could hardly see Gran's house.

"It's *great*!" she shouted up to the crocodile, who was peering over the edge.

"Good," said Gran. "I'll go and fix up the hose pipe."

The lake slowly filled up; slowly, slowly every day the water rose. The crocodile floated happily around in the shallows to begin with, then, as the days went on, he found that he could dive down and spin round and round, just as he had done in his river.

The day the lake was full, a Pook's Prime Pilchards van drew up outside Gran's house.

"One hundred boxes of Prime Pilchard Jelly," said the van driver, "and a tank of fish. Where do you want them, madam?"

"Out the back, please," said Gran.

Moments later there was a loud splash and a scream. Gran rushed round to find Allie pulling the van driver out of the lake and shooing the crocodile away.

"Sorry, Gran," mumbled the crocodile. "It must have been the smell of that jelly stuff. For a moment I thought he was a giant pilchard."

Gran dried out the van driver and sent him on his way.

That evening, Gran, Allie and the crocodile had a lake-warming party. Gran made a fish picnic and a huge plate of pilchard jelly. She also had a surprise for Allie.

"Ooh!" said Allie, when she saw the present wrapped up in fish wrapping paper. "What is it?"

"Open it and see," smiled Gran.

Allie opened it and pulled out a large piece of floppy blue and yellow plastic. "What *is* it, Gran?"

"It's a boat," laughed Gran, "a little dinghy. We'll blow it up and then you can explore the lake and row over to the big island."

Allie was thrilled. "Oh *thank you*, Gran!" She threw her arms around Gran and gave her a big hug.

"No," said Gran. "Thank *you*, dear, for bringing this lovely crocodile to stay with me."

Gran and Allie blew up the boat while the crocodile ate all the pilchard jelly. Then Gran sat happily on the side of her brand new lake and watched Allie and the crocodile chasing each other around the big island.

"Well," Gran said to herself, "this is much more fun than Tibbles ever was."